D1131226

The Old Priest

DRUE HEINZ LITERATURE PRIZE

2013

The Old Priest

Anthony Wallace

University of Pittsburgh Press

Published by the University of Pittsburgh Press,
Pittsburgh, Pa., 15260
Copyright © 2013, Anthony Wallace
All rights reserved
Manufactured in the United States of America
Printed on acid-free paper
10 9 8 7 6 5 4 3 2 1

Library of Congress Cataloging-in-Publication Data

Wallace, Anthony
The Old Priest / Anthony Wallace
pages cm. — (Drue Heinz Literature Prize)
ISBN 978-0-8229-4429-4 (hardcover : acid-free paper)
1. Life change events—Fiction. I. Title.
PS3623.A359744A6 2013
813'.6—dc23   2013023618

To Allene

Contents

The Old Priest

The Old Priest

THE OLD PRIEST IS A JESUIT, BRAINY AND fey. He smokes Pall Malls fixed bayonet-style in an onyx and silver cigarette holder and crosses his legs at the knee. He tells stories as if he is being interviewed for a public television special on old priests. A small, guttural chuckle serves to launch one of his very interesting anecdotes: it's a kind of punctuation that serves as transition, like a colon or dash. You bring your latest girl to see the old priest, you always bring your latest girl to see the old priest.

"Mildred, what are you doing with this rascal?" asks the old priest, ordering a Tanqueray martini "standing up."

Mildred squeals at the idea of you as a rascal. Everything is very jolly. The old priest's hair is the same shade of silver as the end of his cigarette holder, a prop that fascinates Mildred.

"This cigarette holder was given to me by the mother of one of my students," explains the old priest. "She didn't think priests should smoke non-filtered cigarettes, and she objected to the bit of tobacco that became occasionally lodged in the corner of my mouth. Later that same mother, emboldened by one too many grappas, tried to seduce me in the sitting room of the country house where I was to spend the weekend."

Your latest girl is rapt at the stories of the old priest, they are always rapt, the old priest does half the seducing for you.

Back in the room Mildred says, "That's some old priest. Is he gay?"

"What do you think?"

"I think all you Catholic school boys seem gay."

Another girl and the old priest, always ready to be bought lunch or dinner. He smokes, drinks, laughs, tells stories—makes people feel as though they are participating in the history of their own time. The old priest is a monologist of the old school, tossing brightly colored balls into the air and keeping them aloft.

"Another time, we were in Madrid and wanted to get out and see the night life," recalls the old priest. "We concocted a story that the American ambassador had invited us to dinner, but the prefect said that in order to receive permission to leave the house after nine we'd need the permission of the provincial. The provincial said, 'If the American ambassador really wants to see you, he'll invite you to lunch.' My friend Arthur Ramsay thought we were sunk right then and there, but I convinced him that we should go through with it anyway, even though it was against the rules. We danced the flamenco till three."

Everything is very jolly. Your girl is from the South this time and refers to the old priest as a "sexy old queen."

Time and again you meet the old priest. Years fly by the way they used to mark time in the movies: wind and leaves, the corny tearing of the calendar page, the plangent tolling of Time's own iron bell. You either bring a girl along or, if you're depressed, you go by yourself and expect to be consoled.

"I want to write but I can't write," you say.

"It will come," says the old priest. "Give it time. But the pattern is that you should have written your first stories by now. You're a bit behind schedule, you know."

You can almost convince yourself that he knows what he's talking about. He speaks with the authority of a grammar book and is relentlessly optimistic.

2

Life takes you through a couple of twists and turns, you do things you never thought you'd be doing. You live in a rooming house, you drink a lot in the evening, you work a day job as a blackjack dealer in Atlantic City. You wear a white tuxedo, red bow tie and matching red buttons, which your fellow croupiers refer to as "the clown suit." Nobody, not even you, can believe it.

In summer the old priest comes for a visit. You shake martinis in your third floor efficiency. The heat is stifling, oppressive. Through the walls wafts the scent of frying meat, and a loud conversation that goes on and on.

"This is a house of failure," the old priest says, jaunty in his white polo shirt and Madras shorts.

"It's experience."

"So is being bitten by a shark."

"I need a membership card that provides entrée into the historical moment."

"Dear child, I have no idea what you're talking about," the old priest says, pausing for the transitional laugh. "When I was your age I was going to the bullfights in Spain. We actually saw Ava Gardner one time. I went beforehand to ask for permission but the prefect said, 'Jesuits don't go to bullfights.' When we got there the place was crawling with Jesuits in mufti."

In your spare time you read Rimbaud and crave poetry, mystery, illumination. You find an old fish tank somebody has left at the curb and in it, according to the directions of a mail order kit, you raise a crop of hallucinogenic mushrooms. Two weeks before Christmas you visit the old priest at his sister's house on Cape Cod, in Wellfleet, where you plan to spend the weekend breaking into the ancient mysteries. Poetry, mystery, illumination: you'd like to get to the bottom of it.

The old priest says to you as you're unpacking: "Be careful not to leave anything behind. A friend of mine left a pair of black briefs in the guest bed and now my sister says she is beginning to believe everything she reads in the papers."

"Just from a pair of black briefs?"

"Well, apparently he had *Booty on Board* embroidered into the rather narrow seat. Oh dear heavens!"

You drink a pitcher of martinis accompanied by three slices of American cheese and a box of stale Ritz crackers. For dessert you chew the mushrooms, one or two at a time, unsure of the proper dosage.

"This is a fine delicacy," the old priest says. "It's a first-rate cocktail snack."

You nibble the mushrooms, dried and crumbling in your fingertips. The pattern and texture of the desiccated stems and tiny caps become increasingly interesting until, without much warning, the old priest has sprouted tufts of white hair on his face, and his pinkish hands also have sprouted coarse white hair and the hard dull grayish-black points of two cleft hooves.

"Don't look now, but you've turned into a goat-man," you say to the old priest.

"Is that true?" wonders the old priest, lighting a cigarette. Even as a goat-man the old priest has not lost his taste for tobacco.

"Just look for yourself in the mirror."

The old priest stands to look into the gilt-framed mirror that hangs full length above the red velveteen sofa.

"I suppose I have," remarks the old priest, vaguely amused. "Is it permanent, do you think?"

"For the next eight hours or so, anyway." You laugh. The idea of the old priest transformed into a goat-man is hilarious.

He examines himself in the glass, puffing his cheeks and shaking his oversized head. When the cigarette is finished he shakes the cigarette holder and the final few filaments of burning tobacco fall to the floor. He stands before the glass with the empty cigarette holder and begins to wave it in front of him in frantic, cross-like motions.

You take life, but you can't give it," says the old priest, his hand trembling but his eyes fixed steadily forward. "Gangsters," he says, "Cosmic bully-boys—"

"Who are you talking to?" you ask.

"I have to chase these demons away," is his response, but after a few more swipes he sits down on the sofa, places the cigarette holder in his shirt pocket, and laces his fingers together. "We're not supposed to see this," says the old priest, plainly worried. "This is a sin we're committing."

"It's just in our heads," you laugh. "It's the power of the human imagination."

That's what you intend to say but it comes out, *It's the power of the fungus humungination.*

"Oh no it's not," is his answer. "It's even worse for you if you think it is."

He gets down on all fours and in the process the cigarette holder drops suddenly to the ground. He clatters goat-like back and forth in front of you on his knuckles and knees, shaking the walls and knocking his sister's knick-knacks from the mildewed shelves.

"Look what you've done to me now," says the old priest,

goat-like and forlorn. "Look what you've done to me now."

"Where's your God now?" you say, laughing, in your best Edward G. Robinson, then are immediately sorry to have said it. You are sorry to have turned the old priest into a goat-man. You are sorry to have spoiled his religion, to have brought him pagan-low. You are sorry for everything. This is something you've been taught, something that will not go away. You are sorry for *everything*.

The Baltimore Catechism: "O my God I am heartily sorry for having offended Thee, and I detest all my sins, because of Thy just punishments, but most of all because they offend Thee, my God, who art all-good and deserving of all my love. I firmly resolve, with the help of Thy grace, to sin no more and to avoid the near occasions of sin."

"This is a bad trip," you say, then add that it is his religion, not a handful of dried mushrooms, that makes one sorry about everything. Then you are sorry for that, too.

3

You find a new girl, it's been awhile, things have cooled a bit between you and the old priest since the magic mushroom incident. The three of you get dressed up and go to the best French restaurant in Boston, where the old priest is taking a year's sabbatical at a Jesuit house in Cambridge. He is wearing his Roman collar and all signs of the goat-man have vanished. He looks a bit less puffed around the edges, and his sea-glass eyes are sparkling. It occurs to you that the old priest has been consigned to a drying-out facility.

"Wine," the old priest says, lifting a full glass of Nuits-Saint-Georges. "Bringer of *ekstasis* to pagans and Christians alike."

"What's *ekstasis*?" your new girl Ruthie wants to know.

"Well, it's a bit different than ecstasy as you probably know the definition of that word," explains the old priest, and it occurs to you that he is making a pronounced effort not to leer. "It's the state, literally, of standing outside oneself. Of being able to step outside the prison of one's own body, if only for a moment or two. Isn't that what everybody wants, after all?"

"I guess I've never thought about it that way," your new girl admits, leaning in.

"I dined with a Swiss Jesuit one time," the old priest chuckles, passing Ruthie a bite of his Veal Oscar. "He ordered beef and I ordered duck. I wanted a taste of his beef and do you know what he said? He said, 'If you wanted beef, you should have ordered it, and if I wanted duck, I would have ordered it.' Oh dear heavens! The Swiss, well, you know what Harry Lime says: the great product of their civilization, the cuckoo clock!"

"Were you in Europe a long time?" Ruthie asks.

"Seven years. I wanted to stay and earn a doctorate at the Sorbonne, but the Society of Jesus had other plans for me. I came back to Washington just in time for the Kennedy years, which was quite a spectacle."

"What do you know about anti-Semitism in Europe?" Ruthie asks, a bit pointedly.

"The place is crawling with it, I know that much." He puts down his knife and fork. "Once, during my novitiate, I stayed for a time in a Jesuit house in Vienna. This was in the early fifties, not even ten years after the war, and the city looked it, too. The Jesuit house where I was to spend the summer was an old castle with parapets and ramparts, battlements and whathaveyou. In the first few weeks of my stay I made friends with a Jesuit from Argentina. He liked to joke that so many people from this part of the world had relocated to Argentina that he had to come to Vienna for a while, just to balance things out a bit. Father Madero hated the Viennese Jesuits, though. In the evening after supper we used to go up on the roof to smoke and watch the sky change colors, flocks of swallows darting and diving among the chimneys, and one night he pointed down to a side street—I suppose we were up about eight stories—and said, 'There used to be a synagogue down there, where that kiosk is now standing. One night we were all gathered out here after dinner, smoking cigarettes and chatting, and from this roof we watched a group of men come down the street with sticks and bats. They broke every window in that synagogue, then beat the Jews as they tried to run away. And do you know what your fellow Jesuits did?' asked Father Madero. 'Well, I don't suppose there was much they could do,' I offered, for I knew by then that Father Madero hated the Society of Jesus. 'They cheered,' was his reply, and he began clapping and whistling. Dear sweet Jesus."

"An honest man," Ruthie says, and for a few moments nobody says anything.

"An honest man," Ruthie says once more, reaching with her fork for another bite of his Veal Oscar.

The old priest, it seems, will stop at nothing to impress one of your girlfriends.

You go back up to Boston, this time alone. The new girl once again has not worked out and you are feeling depressed, ahistorical.

"I'm feeling depressed, ahistorical," you tell the old priest.

"Well, so you're making a pile of money, anyway," the old priest says, exhaling cigarette smoke.

"Not a pile, exactly."

"If you're not making a really large sum of money, then I don't get it."

"It's a job to do like any job. I'm not writing anything, so what's the difference?"

"What's the difference with anything?" the old priest wants to know. "Are you living your life or are you not?"

"I have no sense of my life as a part of the historical moment."

"*Idiot*," he says, as if the French pronunciation will soften the blow.

"Maybe I should go to graduate school."

"I was a contrary student myself," the old priest says, though you were in fact a very good student, bursting with promise and the will to please. "If they told me to read *Hamlet* I'd read *Macbeth*, and if they told me to read *Macbeth* then I'd read *Hamlet*. My junior year in high school I despised my English teacher. One time I handed in an E. B. White essay on skating in Central Park, except that I changed it to Boston Common. I got a C. I wanted to write E. B. White and tell him he'd gotten a C in high school composition. They kept me back a year, and I started to wise up."

"They kept you back with Cs?"

"There were other factors."

"Such as?"

"Unbridled contempt. They told me I'd never be accepted at an accredited university, so one day at the end of my senior year, only a couple of weeks before graduation, I walked over to Boston College. They asked me where I was going to high school, and when I told them they simply had me sign the forms and I was admitted at once."

4

The old priest, who was built like an oarsman when you first met him, is nicotine-thin. He is in Philadelphia for the time being, visiting with friends and trying to convince his superiors to re-assign him to Boston, where he still has some family in Southie. He eats hardly anything and insists that the second martini be on the table before dinner is ordered. He likes to drink in table-cloth restaurants because it is more seemly than standing at a bar. However, the new smoking regulations land you at a table near the bar most of the time anyway. The bars are noisy and the old priest hears not so well. The evening ends when you get tired of shouting and pantomiming.

The new girl is a red-haired gold digger named Tanya who has the cheek to order beluga caviar whenever the opportuni-ty presents itself. You eat the caviar on toast points and wash it back with iced Russian vodka. The old priest says, "I was once the guest of a woman who took us to a restaurant in Paris where the waiters came out with great crystal trays of caviar in crystal bowls that were somehow illuminated from the bottom. The lights were extinguished, they brought the caviar out in a pro-cession, a long line of waiters holding the trays aloft on their right arms, the bowls rising up, lit by candleflame, unreal."

The red-haired girl sits rapt, convinced she's stumbled onto a pile of money and that the aristocratic bearing of the old priest proves it. However, this is the third or fourth time you've heard this story, and your attention, like the candleflames be-neath the caviar, is quavering.

"The old priest the old priest!" the red-haired girl says, back in the room. "I've never met anybody like that, a character out of a Waugh novel!" The gold digger is a gold digger, but at least she's not an illiterate like some you've brought round. "It's interesting," she says, "the urge toward self-creation. I guess it's what most intelligent people do," she says, then stares at herself in the hotel mirror.

"Whatever happened to the gold digger?" asks the old priest, raising his martini glass. "I liked her. She spent all your money and told you you were a pompous ass when she was through with you."

"The gold digger hit paydirt, packed her shovel. Is off to another dig, I suppose."

"You shouldn't be so hard on women," says the old priest. "It's their nature to be acquisitive."

"You should have it happen to you sometime."

"Oh dear child, if I were not in the Society of Jesus I'd be prey to every manner of boy hustler." He fixes a cigarette in the holder. "As it stands, I have God on my side and they line up to buy *me* dinner."

"God and history," you say.

"They're not exactly the same thing. Tolstoy calls on us to end the false and unnecessary comedy of history and to dedicate ourselves to the simple act of living."

"Joyce calls history a nightmare," is your response.

"I'm inclined to agree with Tolstoy," laughs the old priest, waving his cigarette in the smoky air. "But that's enough about history. Let's talk about eternity for a while!"

5

The next time you see the old priest he is in Washington, living in a Jesuit house in a sketchy part of Capitol Hill. The Boston plan, it seems, has not worked out, but neither of you mentions it.

"I'm teaching slum children how to speak French," says the

old priest. "I must say it's better than working for the man. But what about you? How's the writing going?"

"I haven't written anything in years. A false alarm, I guess."

"A velleity."

"Huh? How's that?"

"A wish for a wish. But what *are* you doing these days?"

"I left the casino business, finally. I'm waiting for my teaching certificate to come through."

"Congratulations, you've finally done something sensible. But don't be like that English teacher I had. He was giving me Cs, so one time I handed in an essay by E. B. White. It was on ice skating, and I changed the location from Central Park to Boston Common. Have I ever told you this one?"

"No, I don't think so."

"He gave me a C. I wanted to write E. B. White and tell him he'd gotten a C in junior composition at Saint Francis Xavier High School."

"I won't be that kind of English teacher."

"Good."

6

A year later there is a female English teacher, and the two of you take the train from Philadelphia to Washington. Her name is Dawn; she is twenty-three years old and very pretty and also economy-minded, the way natural-born high school teachers always are. When the old priest starts talking about caviar she blenches, orders a tossed salad with low-fat dressing.

"The bowls were themselves of carved ice and illuminated from the bottom, luminous in the dark against the black sleeves of the waiters' jackets and the gleaming white of the doubled cuffs."

"Such extravagance," Dawn says. "Another time in history."

"The woman who threw that party became attached to a gigolo from Argentina who used her, took her money, and left her addicted to prescription drugs."

"Now *that's* a good story," Dawn says.

The old priest comes to Atlantic City for the wedding, even though you've insisted on a civil ceremony, and the two of you have a bachelor party at one of the casino buffets.

"I remember the last day of my first year at Boston College," the old priest tells you, exhaling cigarette smoke. "Have I told you this story?"

"I don't think so."

"My friend Pat Dempsey was waiting for me in a car with the top down. I went into the office and there was this Jesuit behind a desk and I said, 'I want to sign up here. I want to sign up now.' He told me to finish college first, and I told him that if he did not get me right then and there, on that particular day and time of day, he would not get me at all."

"What did he do?"

"He signed me up at once."

"So why didn't you just turn away?"

"It's a vocation. That's what I'm trying to tell you about: something you absolutely have to do, regardless of what anybody thinks. You have no choice in the matter. Like you with your writing."

"But I don't write—I haven't written anything for some time now. I told you before. I stopped all that."

"You're young yet. It will come to you. You can make a pile of money in the casino business and then retire."

"That's what I'm planning on, yes. I'm considering teaching high school English after I retire. What do you think?"

"That's good, as long as you leave yourself time to write."

"I think I can work it in."

"Sink roots down like the roots of old trees."

At the reception the old priest tells stories to Dawn's parents.

"My friend Itchy and I wanted to go to the movies but you had to go to Confession on Saturday nights, so Itchy said to my mother, 'He can go to Confession in my neighborhood, it's on the way to the movie house.' On the way we met this girl Itchy knew and she said, 'Suckenfuckenickel.' I said, 'What?' And she said, 'Suckenfuckenickel.' As we walked away I said to Itchy, 'What did that girl just say to us?' What she'd said was that she would suck and fuck us for a nickel. Oh, dear heavens! Then Itchy took me to his church and pointed to a confessional box and I went in. There was an old German priest in there and he said, 'Who ist das? Is you boy or girl? Speak up! Speak up!' Oh, it was dreadful. I told him my small few sins and he cried, 'Oh you bad boy, oh you wery bad boy!' and began to beat his hands violently against the wooden walls of the confessional box. When I came out Itchy was standing in the vestibule of the church, leaning one elbow against a holy water font and roaring with laughter. We went to the movie but could not contain ourselves. Every time there was a break in the dialogue one of us would shout, 'Oh you bad boy! Oh you wery bad boy!' The third time we started up, the usher came and threw us out the fire door."

"Where'd you get that old priest?" Dawn's mother asks when you come back from the honeymoon.

"He was my French teacher in high school. French and senior guidance. We've stayed in touch."

"He's a scream," Dawn's mother says.

"He is that."

"You should take a page or two out of his book," Dawn's mother suggests.

7

A year later you go down to Washington by yourself. Your English teacher, you've just found out, is having an affair with the school nurse—a pair of lipstick lesbians is the word in the halls—and you want to be consoled. The old priest seldom leaves his room, which reeks of tobacco and is heaped with dirty clothes and cardboard boxes. Wads of crumpled Kleenex are strewn about the floor and heaped atop the dresser. His hair is greenish in a certain light, and his eyeballs and fingertips are different shades of yellow. He wears a mauve crewneck sweater, loose black corduroys, and bedroom slippers with the toes snipped off. His knees, as he stands for a moment to greet you, open and close stiffly as a churchyard gate.

"This is my last weekend in this room," explains the old priest. "They're moving me to assisted living. Father Lemmon was behind it. I helped him through his novitiate and this is the thanks I get. But I shall die as I have lived, safe within the arms of the Society of Jesus!"

You bring Chinese takeout from around the corner and almost get mugged on your way back to the rectory. You set up all the little cartons on his desk, festive as can be, but he barely takes a bite. His hearing has dimmed considerably, and to communicate with him you have to shout. Tufts of coarse white hair sprout from his nose and ears.

"My wife is a lipstick lesbian," you shout.

"How's the cat?" is the old priest's reply.

"I have dogs."

"How are the dogs, then?"

"Fine."

He stares at you, blinks, stares some more.

"I said they're fine. The dogs are just fine."

"Dear child, why are you shouting?"

"I'm passionate about my dogs."

"How's the writing?" the old priest asks.

"I haven't done any writing since I was a young man."

"But you're a young man still."

"That's a matter of opinion, but whatever the case I haven't done any writing for quite some time."

"Well then, how's the casino business?"

"I got out of it years ago. I teach English at Atlantic High. 'Stopping by Woods on a Snowy Evening,' that sort of thing."

"There you are, I knew you'd come to your senses. And you've had children?"

"No, not yet. Maybe soon."

"Don't wait too long: you'll shorten the time you have with your grandchildren."

"That's a point."

"My brother got married at fifty, a very Irish thing to do. He died when his only daughter was still in her teens."

"I didn't know you had a brother."

"Oh, I had two of them, one still alive."

"Why did you never say anything about them?"

"How's that?"

"Why did you never tell me you had two brothers?"

"I don't suppose it ever came up. But Itchy was more like a real brother to me anyway."

"Whatever became of Itchy?"

"Have I not told you that story? Itchy's mother ran off with a man who arranged a ménage à trois between himself, the mother, and the daughter. Itchy stayed with his father, who became very bitter and drank all the time. I think he beat poor Itchy. I came to the door one time and Itchy said, 'Oh, it's you again. Go 'way,' he said, and I went away. I never saw him again."

"Why do you think he did that?"

"He was embarrassed by the situation, I suppose."

"That his father beat him?"

The old priest gazes at you, and again you realize you have to speak up. *"He didn't want people to know his father was beating him?"*

"That I loved him." The old priest leans forward to take your free hand, the hand not holding the drink, in his own two hands. He sits peering at you as if by lantern light. "Dear sweet beautiful child of light and grace. He was embarrassed that I loved him."

8

You picture the old priest in his ritual garments, his "vestments," lifting the host up high at the Consecration, the process of transubstantiation, the moment when a dry disc of unleavened bread becomes the body of Jesus Christ.

Per omnia saecula saeculorum.

Amen.

Pax Domini sit semper vobiscum.

Et cum spiritu tuo.

You picture the old priest in Europe in the fifties, spotting Ava Gardner at a bullfight in Madrid. She is wearing a beret, he is wearing a soutane. This is history. No, wait, he is not wearing a soutane, he is wearing mufti. He is in history and he will lead you into the promised land of the historical moment, the instant in time in which history is happening and you are in history, you yourself present in that unique and meaningful moment: the moment in time when everything makes sense.

This is only theoretical, of course, but even so it seems clear enough to you that there are those who stand inside history and those who stand outside, like beggars at the gate. This is not a matter of money; it is a matter of something else, though it is hard to say exactly what. Whatever it is, though, the old priest seems to have plenty for everyone.

To penetrate time you must go outside of time. Outside of time is the world of myth, of eternal and meaningful recurrence. Even as the old priest tells his anecdotes again and again they acquire substance, a kind of permanence or narrative integrity that goes beyond their literal level. No longer does the old priest as a young boy simply knock at Itchy's door; he eternally knocks at Itchy's door. Itchy, perhaps having just come from a fresh beating, eternally answers the door. This is a cool trick. You'd like to try it yourself, but you keep steady contact with so few people that there aren't many whom you could repeat your stories to, if you had any stories you considered worth repeating. Well, you do, as it turns out. The stories of the old priest.

9

You call the book *The Old Priest* and you get an agent interested, and he gets a publisher interested. Priests old and otherwise are hot news that year because of the sex abuse scandal that is in all the headlines. In the popular imagination priests are rapidly becoming synonymous with pedophiles.

"I like the way you leave the whole sex thing ambiguous,"

your editor says. "That's really the heart of the matter. The idea
of the priest as traditionally representing good is juxtaposed
against the current idea or perception of the priest as representing evil. And you walk the fine line down the middle. Very
'Young Goodman Brown' of you. And of course your character
is destroyed the same way as Young Goodman Brown. We don't
know what or how much really happened. It could all be in his
head. Was there sex between the main character and the old
priest?" the editor wants to know. "I mean, just between us."

"I don't know. I left it up in the air, so I never really had to
make that decision."

"Smart. Play both ends against the middle."

The Old Priest is a short novel that was formatted and mar-
keted as a novel, on the supposition that some people would like
to say they've read a novel but not spend a lot of time actually
reading one. It is written in the second person; it is "mannered,
overstylized, derivative," to quote one reviewer. As a writer you
have some talent, most people seem to agree, but you also have
an odd quirk that has proven a fairly severe limitation: you are
only truly comfortable writing in the second person.

In fact, you wanted to change the title of your book to *The
Second Person*, but the publisher didn't want to do it and the
book went out into the world as *The Old Priest*.

"Old priests are what sell," the editor told you, "not witty ref-
erences to grammar books and Graham Greene. Let your character be the sap and you be the smart one."

He was smart, that editor, but he missed the reference to
Jesus, the second person of the Holy Trinity. Also perhaps the
second person as the conscience or moral self, now that you
think of it. (Can the self be parsed out grammatically? The self

of the first person, the self of the second person, and the self of
the third person? Our own interior Holy Trinity?) All the same,
you liked that: "Grammar Books and Graham Greene" really
should be the title of something, though nothing you will ever
write.

10

Somewhere along the line it occurs to you that you should let
the old priest know you've written a book about him. Well not
about him, exactly, but a book in which he served as the artist's
model. You don't, though; something stops you whenever you
think about it.

The last time you saw him was right after Father Lemmon
had him moved to the assisted living facility outside Baltimore,
and the room and his condition were even more depressing
than they'd been when he was fending for himself in the Jesuit
house on Capitol Hill.

"They seem to have taken the assistance out of assisted living," you observed dryly.

"They come in once a week to give me a shower, shave me,
comb my hair. Then I sit here for a week, smoking and doing
crossword puzzles, until they come back again. I get a carton
of cigarettes and some books, two meals a day brought to this
room. Oh dear sweet Jesus." No irony, no dry twist: no guttural
colon or dash.

"Are you getting any visitors? Any family members dropping in?"

"My brother Jack came by two weeks ago and brought me a
crab cake," said the old priest, and gave you a sharp look.

He also mentioned the name of former student X, who'd arrived the week before with a six-pack of beer, drank all six cans,

then went off to the National Gallery for an afternoon of Vermeer. You've dined with former student X on a few occasions, have even bought him dinner once or twice. He is one of those people who are always working on their dissertations. Sometimes if you came with a new girl the old priest would bring former student X. You always wondered if he and the old priest were having an affair, although that might not be the right term. Illicit sex, in any case, since priests young and old take a vow of celibacy, and also since homosexual behavior is considered sinful by the very organization which the old priest claims to represent. At these dinners there would always be too much drinking, and sometimes former student X would sit across the table and leer at you in the manner of a gothic double, your very own William Wilson. He is six or seven years younger than you, athletic, not as bright as you but possessing an ingenuousness the old priest seemed to consider a highly valuable quality: an ingenuousness that liked to flirt with disingenuousness. The old priest would frequently say about former student X, "Oh, he is like a big kid! Oh, he is like a big big kid!" You asked one time, rather pointedly, why big-kiddedness should be such a desirable quality, but the old priest waved the question away with a puff of cigarette smoke and the hoarse, watery laugh. "Oh dear heavens!" he laughed. "Oh dear heavens!"

It occurred to you in the assisted living facility outside Baltimore that you would be happy to see former student X never again.

II

The old priest appears to you in a dream. He is eating duck liver pâté and drinking a glass of Meursault. The grayish-brown pâté froths at the corners of his mouth. Then he turns into a goat-man, cloven hooves and wispy white fur on his hands and cheeks. Then he uses the cigarette holder to subdue the goat-man. When you wake up you think you finally know the secret of the old priest, but as the day wears on you see that you were mistaken. The idea of the old priest is a mass of sticky contradictions and reversals.

The old priest is a kind and gentle man, a generous and considerate friend. The old priest is a pedophile who enjoys the company of high school boys or their equivalent. The old priest is old as sin. The old priest is witty as redemption.

12

In the Catholic grammar school you attended as a boy the priests kept themselves at a distance while the nuns ran the show, dour and plentiful in their identical costumes, as if they'd tumbled out of a machine that vended them a penny apiece. If a priest came into the classroom on the odd Tuesday afternoon it was like Jesus Christ almighty had come down from the cross to tell a few jokes or riddles. One priest was a fanatic for spelling, another asked questions plucked randomly from the Baltimore Catechism.

Who made us?

God made us.

Who is God?

God is the Supreme Being who made all things.

And so on.

Another priest, an older man, the pastor, came into the classroom a few times a year and claimed to be able to read everyone's thoughts. As he went through the catalog of what all the children were thinking, he threw his arms around and paced violently, in the manner of Bishop Sheen. He scared the bejesus out of you, you have to admit. Then too, that was the whole point.

At a certain time of year the parish priest came to bless the house. You remember your grandmother kneeling down in the cramped living room, her head bowed, the priest intoning the words and sending sprinklets of holy water flying from a small, occult-looking bottle drawn from his inside pocket. You like to remember his black suit, his black hat with its short brim, his small black cigar balanced nimbly on the railing just beyond the open doorway. The priest reeking of cigar smoke and spewing holy water on the dated furniture. Your grandmother kneeling on the spinach-colored carpet, kerchiefed head bowed low. Years later this memory or set of memories was triggered by the climactic scene in *The Exorcist*: the two priests standing in the room with the possessed girl, throwing holy water and chanting, "The power of Christ compels you! The power of Christ compels you!"

There have been other movies, other movie priests:

Pat O'Brien as Father Jerry Connelly, the slum priest who has turned away from a life of crime in *Angels with Dirty Faces*.

Bing Crosby and Barry Fitzgerald in *Going My Way*.

Bing Crosby once again as kindly and melodious Father O'Malley in *The Bells of St. Mary's*.

Spencer Tracy as fighting Father Flanagan in *Boys Town*.

David Niven as the ambitious but unhappy Episcopal bishop in *The Bishop's Wife* (helped to a deeper level of spirituality by Cary Grant's angel Dudley).

Karl Malden as the two-fisted activist priest in *On the Waterfront*.

Oskar Werner as the tormented and dying theologian in *The Shoes of the Fisherman*. Also in that same movie Anthony Quinn as the pope who opens the coffers of the Roman Catholic Church to the world's poor and hungry. The pope, don't forget, is also a priest (he roams the streets of Rome, gives tender counsel to an English woman whose marriage to David Jansen is on the rocks).

A not very well-known actor as the priest in *The Song of Bernadette* who believes Jennifer Jones has had a true vision of the Blessed Virgin Mary. (The same actor played the father-in-law in *Days of Wine and Roses*, if that is any help.)

Rex Harrison as the pope who commissions the painting of the Sistine Chapel in *The Agony and the Ecstasy*.

Tom Tryon, before he became a novelist, in *The Cardinal*.

Richard Chamberlain as the priest with the untamable lust in *The Thorn Birds*.

Robert De Niro as the priest who tries to play the complicated game of church politics in *True Confessions*.

William S. Burroughs as the junkie priest in *Drugstore Cowboy*.

There should be more movie priests, priests we have yet to see upon the silver screen.

The priest who solicits oral sex in the sacristy, then absolves the altar boy when he is finished with him. *Absolvo te* blah blah blah. There has never been a language better than Latin when it comes to being an old priest. Mysterious, arcane, dripping of the long ago.

The cheerful parish priest who lives a decent life, ministers to his flock, likes to treat himself to a good dinner, likes even better to be treated by his well-heeled parishioners. He is affable, physically soft, a guy who knows how to go along to get along.

The priest lost in the mysticism of his own religion, sitting alone in his room, chanting gibberish. If he were not a priest he would be on the street, living in a cardboard box. His illness is legitimized, yet who is to say he is not a true mystic? Then too, who is to say the guy living in the cardboard box is also not a true mystic?

The priest who leaves his order and breaks his vows to marry the woman he met working behind the counter in the pizza shop. The priest who leaves his order to marry the nun he met in the grammar school. The priest who leaves his order to marry the priest he met in the seminary or, much later perhaps, the one who reminds him of that charming young fellow.

There was an old woman, one time, the grandmother of a high school acquaintance, who said that you should be a priest, you had just the right look. You pretended to wonder what she meant by that, but you knew exactly what she meant by that.

You are sitting in a bar in downtown Atlantic City on a weekday afternoon.

"The Catholic Church," somebody says.

"Yeah, the Catholic Church," somebody replies.

"The Gay and Lesbian Society of North America," the first man sniggers.

"So it would seem," is the only thing you can say.

"They take their training in the *semenary*," another man chortles.

"They're just like anybody else," someone else says.

"But they say not," another man, all the way down at the end, puts in. "They say they're in the know."

"Who says that?"

"*They* say. They themselves."

"Someone should be in the know, shouldn't they?" you wonder out loud.

"Sure," the first man says. "But we all know nobody is."

13

The old priest no longer answers his phone, he does not have voice mail, he does not have e-mail. A few years go by, a few years then a few years more.

Once, when *The Old Priest* was first published, you did a reading at a Barnes and Noble in Philadelphia and former student X turned up, leering at you from the back of the room.

"This is great," said former student X, coming forward after the reading to have his copy of the book signed. "This is absolutely fantastic."

"Thanks. I guess my writing has finally come to something, though I'm not expecting much from this financially."

"Does he know?"

"Who?"

"Who!"

"Oh, well, no, I've lost track of him, actually. He's become fairly reclusive, it seems." Then you looked at the book in former student X's hand, the book jacket with its illustration taken from the Baltimore Catechism, the three milk bottles that illustrate the soul in its various states: the full milk bottle is the state of grace, the empty milk bottle is mortal sin, the milk bottle with some spots in it is venial sin: heaven, hell, purgatory.

"Oh—oh, I see—you're jumping to conclusions there, but of course I can see the impulse. I can definitely understand—"

"He mentioned you, you know," said former student X. "Last time I was down there, in that terrible place in Baltimore. He was wondering why he never hears from you anymore."

"Oh, was he, now? I'll have to be sure and give him a call and tell him all about this, though of course the character of the old priest is a composite of a lot of priests I've known over the years. Some that are now in jail, actually!"

You broke into a loud, obnoxious laugh then moved to sign the flyleaf of your book for the next person in line.

That was the last time you saw former student X, thank God.

14

After his novitiate in Europe the old priest came back to run a Jesuit high school in Georgetown, beginning in the early sixties, the Kennedy years through "We Shall Overcome" and "Burn, Baby, Burn" right into the middle of Watergate, the old priest always one to stand with both feet planted squarely in the historical moment. He came to Philadelphia in the fall of '73, he was your senior guidance counselor and also became your French teacher when the original Jesuit who was your French teacher left midyear to marry a woman he'd met in a pizza shop. Those were somewhat different times, the seventies, when a man might suddenly drop whatever he was doing and run off with a woman he'd met in a pizza shop. (Of course that is still possible, but it no longer seems quite so commonplace.) Love was in the air, also anxiety, depression, the mounting dread brought on by Vietnam, Nixon and Watergate, Black Power and Women's Rights, the death of the patriarchy that seemed likely to accompany the gradual breakdown in faith in

government and religious institutions, a return to individual-
ity and the pleasure principle, the inevitable victory of subjec-
tivity and moral relativism, blah blah *blah*—

You remember how he seduced you, the old priest, how he
charmed the David Bowie pants off you. Maybe that was part
of it: '73, David Bowie and Rod Stewart, a little later Mott the
Hoople and Queen: androgyny was just then having its fifteen
minutes. The David Bowie pants? Oh, well, they came up really high at the waist and then billowed out in an exaggerated
three pleat, descending to two-inch cuffs designed to go with
platform shoes. You had two pairs of each, an incongruously
apt style for a skinny seventeen-year-old prep school student,
it lasted about fifteen minutes.

One day the two of you smoking cigarettes in his office after
hours he told you all about William Peter Blatty and the young
Jesuits of Georgetown, in a smoky pub one afternoon mer-
rily gathered round a mongrel-brown Lester spinet. Stories
were told. Information was leaked. Classified material about
the Devil got out. There really was an exorcism, though it was
performed on a Lutheran boy by not one or two but an entire
team of exorcists. The exorcism itself went on for months, the
whole thing audio taped and the tapes themselves locked away
in some vault in the Vatican.

The best parts of the book, according to the old priest—the
best parts, of course, being the scariest parts—were taken directly from the secret transcripts. He knew people who knew people
who knew the Devil! Talk about being on the inside track!

The old priest told his stories—he always told stories—
which meant of course that he had stories to tell. You fell in
love, *whatever that means*, can you just admit that much? People fall in love: kids and old ladies, middle-aged bachelors and
hot young kindergarten teachers. The heart has its own secret

life, like the family cat, and what it might drag home is any-body's guess.

Not love, perhaps, but a schoolboy crush. Something glandular but at the same time completely non-glandular.

Can you admit *that* much?

Of course you can. Sometimes. Once in a while.

15

You remember your childhood, the lower-middle-class Irish neighborhood in South Philadelphia, the corner tap rooms with their blacked-out windows, Krause's bakery each Sunday morning after eight o'clock Mass. You remember polishing your shoes for Easter Sunday, the church the next morning filled with fresh white lilies, the pews and the side aisles, all along the stations of the cross, overflowing with parishioners there to perform their "Easter duty," which is another way of saying that they didn't go very often but neither did they wish their membership to lapse.

When you were eight years old you watched *The Song of Bernadette*, in rerun, on your grandmother's black-and-white Motorola. You looked up at the dark place at the top of the stairs, hoping that the Blessed Virgin Mary would suddenly appear to you. Wanting that to happen more than anything else in this world. Also not wanting that to happen more than anything else in this world.

You think sometimes of the candy store lady, whose response to everything was JesusMaryandJoseph JesusMaryandJoseph JesusMaryandJoseph JesusMaryandJoseph JesusMaryandJoseph JesusMaryandJoseph.

One day a punk of the neighborhood came barreling into

the store and knocked your pinball machine on tilt. You backed
down, of course, the boy took your machine, and the old woman sent up a fervent chorus of JesusMaryandJoseph Jesus-
MaryandJoseph JesusMaryandJoseph JesusMaryandJoseph
JesusMaryandJoseph JesusMaryandJoseph.

Then there was the time with the little girl in the alleyway, ex-
posing yourselves as little children sometimes do. You were
both five: tiny Adam and miniature Eve. The girl, you've heard,
has grown up to be a junkie, a prostitute, a queen of the do-
it-yourself porn industry. "Her name was Grace," you say out
loud. Her name *is* Grace, you correct yourself, though not out
loud. But you don't know if she is among the living or the dead.

16

One time, very drunk, as drunk as the two of you have ever
been together, the old priest said: "I send this one out to live in
the world. This is the one you see. You like this one. But you
wouldn't like the other one."
"How do you know?"
"Trust me, you wouldn't."
"Just give me a peek."
"I'm afraid I can't do that. He can't be trusted. No, I'm afraid
it's absolutely out of the question. He's locked up safe and sound
as The Man in the Iron Mask. Ha ha."
You went home, thinking of the real old priest bound and
tossed into a dungeon, the iron mask locked securely to con-
ceal his face, the brutal, ignorant guards to glimpse only his
wry mouth and sea-glass eyes. Of course the question then
becomes which old priest is out in the world and which one

locked away? It occurred to you then and has crossed your mind a few times since that the old priest is an archfiend, an imposter who walks the earth while the true old priest—well, it's too horrible to imagine.

Years later you realize that you've done much the same thing with the old priest, or rather with the simulacrum of the old priest. He imprisoned the real old priest while you imprisoned the fake one. He's in a book you wrote called *The Old Priest*. He's in there, drinking Tanqueray martinis and telling his charming anecdotes. He's locked up, safe and sound.

17

The Old Priest, as it turns out, pretty quickly became a period piece. It went almost at once to the remainder tables, probably due to its lack of explicitness. Old priests are what sell, but only if you catch them *en flagrante*. Once in a while you take a peek at the book yourself. It is not very good. It is "mannered," as one reviewer pointed out, and it is also derivative, a retelling of the old priest's stories combined with some mildly ambiguous hints at homosexuality, a strange and self-conscious amalgamation of *The Power and the Glory* and *Brideshead Revisited* by way of *A Separate Peace* and *The Trouble with Angels*.

It is as outmoded as those lace things they used to place on the tops of parlor chairs so that one's head wouldn't stain the fabric. Why would one's head stain the fabric? Hair oil, perhaps, or dye the color and consistency of shoe polish. The old priest would know what those things are called, were called. But you don't, although among your students it is well known that when asked your favorite book your immediate response is the *OED*. Nobody, not even your colleagues, seems to re-

member that that was Auden's famous reply. You've got your
tweed, your manners and your mannerisms, a few chestnuts in
the one hand, a couple of shibboleths in the other.

Still, it was your dream, publishing a novel, the dream of
your youth, and since you have a novel, albeit one that has not
done very well and is currently out of print (alas), you now have
a job, comfortable enough, in which you will live out the rest
of your days, professionally speaking. Teaching English in a
posh New England boarding school, well talk about mannered!
Tweeds, rep ties. For a joke on the first day of school you sometimes wear a boater!

And so once again you are back in Boston, this time without
the old priest, a strange and portentous reversal to have ended
up where he would like to be but is not. You are getting on in
years, living by yourself in a large but shabby one-bedroom on
Washington Street, the bedroom itself facing the street so that
you have to protect your sleep with a white noise machine or
an air conditioner, depending on the time of year. The white
noise machine, which looks like something designed for a low-
budget sci-fi movie, sounds like the endless slosh and chop of
some eternal ocean. The air conditioner sounds like the void:
empty and metallic, within its steady whoosh the pock and
ping of atoms whirling into extinction.

Whatever has become of the gaiety of the old priest? Sitting
at a dinner table, enraptured with the present moment, seeing
and being seen, fine clothes and expensive bar drinks and first
class victuals, all of life's possibilities laid out before you like
a flight of oysters. Now you are getting old and have resigned
yourself to bachelorhood. Your talent, paltry at its best, has left
you; you walk the cold streets of Beantown in shabby clothes, a
denizen of the pubs and secondhand book stores.

Your students like you all the same. You are an affable old failure who is nevertheless a tough old bird, an eagle's eye for the misplaced comma and the misused semicolon: some of the hipper students call you "Old School" behind your back, or you wish they would. The truth is you give them all Bs, and the girls with pert breasts get B plusses. Oh, even the girls without pert breasts get B plusses, who are you kidding? The poor sad pimply-faced freshman boys, arms and legs askew, get the B minuses, and they deserve them, too. They themselves admit as much.

"Walk among them," advised the old priest when he found out you'd become a high school English teacher. "Always teach standing up. Be a presence among them. Let them feel your presence as you walk among them."

You walk among your own students and wish to tousle their hair or to trail your fingers across their downy arms as they sit, scribbling in their notebooks. And what would be so wrong in that?

In your free time you tinker with a second novel, which you call *The Western Gate* after a line from "Luke Havergal." These days if you can only get to twenty thousand words they'll package it some way to make it look like a novel, or at least they will if they think they can sell it that way. *The Western Gate* is the story of a dissipated novelist, a drunk and a womanizer who is his own worst enemy. He drinks, adulterizes, insults powerful people while going about his drinking and adulterizing. Once again the material is a combination of thinly veiled biography and heavy-handed fantasy. You use the details of your own boarding school and place within those details yourself as an idealized creation, a writer talented but with a checkered past and an unreliable conscience. You yourself have neither—at least not to a degree anybody would find interesting. You have never adulterized, have rarely insulted anyone, and go quietly home from the pub after two pints. You have no illusions about leading your students into the promised land of the historical moment; in fact, you have no illusions about anything at all.

18

Life goes on this way—wind and leaves, the corny tearing of the calendar page—until one October afternoon, after explaining to your AP seniors the theological underpinnings of "Everything that Rises Must Converge," you go to check your e-mail and there is death—exactly where you expected it would be.

> (Salutation,)
>   I am sad to inform you Fr. passed away. He has a viewing this evening in Philadelphia and then a mass tomorrow morning at St. Ignatius Church in Baltimore and then afterward is being buried at the Woodstock cemetery, also in Baltimore.
>   I think of you often, and gather you are a quite successful writer.
>   Be well,
>   (Former Student X)

19

You write back, describing what you were doing on the day of the old priest's passing—the conversation you had with your students about "the world of guilt and sorrow" just moments before reading of the old priest's death—expressing regret that you were not present and asking the obvious questions. What you really want are the details that will allow you to form a resolution—the resolution that will allow you to close the book.

(Salutation,)

The viewing was in Philadelphia at Manresa Hall on Friday, October 27th. A place for old and dying priests. There were about 10 really old priests in walkers and wheelchairs, as well as former student Y and former student Z and myself from the class of 1982. There was also one gentleman from Gonzaga's class of 1961, who is an architect in Bryn Mawr now, and one other impaired middle-aged man present. I overheard the gentleman with a short leg and hearing aid tell another priest that when he was at Georgetown Prep he was bullied because of a speech impediment and his limp, and Fr. helped put an end to it. The day was cloudy, cold, and drizzling wet. After the viewing he was taken to Baltimore. Fr. Lemmon did the ceremony (I was not there) at St. Ignatius Church. Apparently, there is a Woodstock cemetery in Baltimore, and that is where he will be buried.

As for not seeing him...no one knew how sick he was. I saw him in mid-September. My wife Susan (I recently got married) and I went to the Provincial's House in Baltimore where he was living and took him out for lunch. We showed him our wedding pictures. Of course he had his cigarettes and martini. He was frail. When I inquired to his health, as I always did, he said "not bad for a man of my age, don't you think?"

In early October, he was sent to Manresa Hall in Philadelphia. They could not care for him at the Provin-

cial's House in Baltimore any longer; for the last year he
had been struggling with throat and neck cancer. Yet not
even his sister and niece, nor anyone close to him knew
until a week or two before he died. He was in Philadelphia, 15 minutes away from me, and I did not even know.
His sister remarked that it was the typical Irish way,
not to talk about illness and dying. That is all she could
understand of not knowing, and she would be likely to
do the same, if she was dying.

As for "the world of guilt and sorrow," remember
Flannery O'Connor also said "All is sacred, nothing
profane," and as Fr. used to quote to me from St. Julian
of Norwich, "All shall be well, and all shall be well, and
all manner of thing shall be well." Fr. would not want us
to spend any useless time on guilt and sorrow.

In the last month, the cancer became extremely aggressive, and he developed a large tumor on his neck
and left chin. It was visible, although I did not see it a
month ago. On his last day, Friday, October 20th, he got
up, although hard to eat and talk at this point. He got
dressed. At lunch went outside to smoke and had a drink
while reading the *New York Times*. After lunch he told
the head nurse he was going to take a nap. She went in
to check on him, because that was not typical, and after
a time, he appeared to wake up abruptly, got halfway
up from the bed, looked her way, collapsed to his side
and died. He went without pain, quickly, doing what he
loved—smoking, drinking, and reading. He said to me,
he thought of death as a perfectly open door, with bright
light radiating, and that one day he would casually walk
through the door. He also told me he cared about this

life, and that he did not give a shit about death because it was completely unknowable.

It is particularly strange that you were teaching Flannery O'Connor and the underpinnings of theology. I am sitting here with Fr.'s Master's Thesis from Louvain completed April 2, 1954, entitled "Theology and Prayer."

In it Fr. writes, "A book is a machine to think with. In a good book this statement is verified both for the reader and writer alike. I do not flatter myself that this short paper offers that advantage to any reader it may have. My problem is too personal, as is the solution I have worked out for myself. This paper is a nothing more than a machine for thinking out a problem that has long troubled me. It were better compared to a loom upon which I propose to weave some of the unraveled elements of science, service, and prayer. My problem in its simplest form was this: how to integrate the elements of prayer, theology, and daily routine into a unified whole? Or more exactly, what is the point at which theology can become the living source, the principle of prayer and action? If such a point of insertion existed, and I did not for a moment doubt that it did, I wanted to find it and to formulate it as accurately as possible. Because, above all, my solution had to be a practical solution. I wanted a principle that would be operative beyond the walls of the Theologate, that would prolong, not only the effects of our four years of study, but would keep theology as the central point of reference from which all flowed and to which all returned, so that no phase of my life as a priest would not know its permeating presence. I think I have found such a principle in that method of theologi-

cal reasoning we call the 'Argumentum ex Convenientia.' I look upon the 'Argumentum ex Convenientia' as
the summit of theological reasoning, that towards which
all the rest of theology is ultimately oriented; and I find
that it is at the same time a form of prayer, a method, if
you want to place it in a category, which partakes of the
nature of contemplation.

"If the objection were raised at this point that I am
assigning too large a place to Theology in the life of
prayer, that the spiritual life can be lived on the highest
level without any reference, explicit at least, to theology,
I would reply that although this might be true, it should
not be true in the case of a Jesuit."

Fr. goes on to say that "To highlight one aspect of this
interdependence of Theology and Sanctity is my purpose here." Much of the writing is in French and hence I
am unable to translate, given my poor skills as a French
student. There is another passage I think you would
like, a few pages on, in which Father talks about eternity
as a place that contains everything that has ever been,
every lost dog, as he describes it, every broken watch
and burnt dinner, then adds, "If eternity really is eternity,
then nothing is ever lost. It's all there, for all time, safe
and whole within the sight of God. This in itself is the
'living source' that Theology describes and that prayer
allows us to stand in daily relation to and which, properly understood, is the source of meaningful action."

As for my life, I am a tenure track assistant professor
of counseling at Community College of Philadelphia.
I love my work. I hear Fr. in my work every day as a

teacher and counselor. I got married in June and live in Collingswood, New Jersey with my wife Susan, a medical writer from a Nebraska farm of strong willed German stock. She has a Ph.D. in food science and an MBA, was in the Peace Corps in Ghana, and lived in Tunisia for a year doing research. She is a fascinating woman, and she makes me a better man.

I struggle every day with good and evil in my life, but it is a worthy fight. I am not a very good Christian or Catholic, but I never give up the fight. Sometimes I make the fight harder than it needs to be, but I guess I fight better as an underdog.

Life is beautiful, fleeting and tragic, and I love every minute of it.

I have attached a picture of Father a little less than a year before he died, and a wedding picture. I picture Father now at this moment frolicking among the lost dogs and broken watches and burnt dinners of Eternity.

I hope you are well. Thank You.

Your brother through Christ,

(Former Student X)

20

In Maytime of a certain year, in the auditorium of your Catholic grammar school, you attended a vocational fair hosted by the Maryknoll Fathers, who are missionaries. You saw a glossy illustration of a Maryknoll Father who'd been tortured by savages, and you got an erotic charge. In the same week you read *Dracula*, which was your favorite novel until *The Scarlet Letter* came along a few years later. In Maytime of a certain year you began to see the connection between sex and death. Sex is sin is death. Then, as you continued to look, it really got confusing. Sex is sin is death is the resurrection and the life.

The old priest: "Once, in that Jesuit house in Vienna, I found a room that was like a medieval torture chamber. There were whips and straps, iron benches and wooden racks. Good heavens!"

"But why would anybody want to do such things?"

"To abase the flesh, of course."

"But why would you want to do *that?*"

"*Idiot.*"

"Did you try it?"

"I went in there one afternoon, the room completely empty and still, sunlight coming in through the barred windows and the little chinks in the wall, and I thought of Itchy, and I flogged my bare back mercilessly for one hour. There are some things lost to us in modern times that ought not to be lost. Many things, actually, that most people would call barbaric, or medieval, but ideas and practices we might need all the same. Things lost to us that we can't do without, even if we don't know we can't do without them."

In the end you are alone, a bachelor-teacher at a posh New England boarding school. Not the worst life you could have imagined for yourself, though a suite of rooms at the boarding school would be better than taking the train each morning from North Station. Your colleagues are entertained to no end with the stories of your colorful past, the casino days of your profligate youth. Oh, how they wish they had lived such a varied and adventurous life!

In the end you are alone in your room, still thinking of the old priest, what to say about your friendship, your "relationship," what not to say, how to write an end to this, if the ending is yours to write. As a young man you were awkward and depressed, youthfully morbid but far from Keatsian. Women found you dull, ponderous—"bloodless," as one of the cleverer ones observed from the other side of an open doorway—intelligent but without much style or imagination. The old priest alone took an interest in you. Years later you read a few newspaper articles that caused you to see this overweening interest in a somewhat different light.

In the rooming house in Atlantic City where you settled down after college the old priest came for a visit that very first summer, jaunty in his white polo shirt and Madras shorts. You sat up all night smoking cigarettes and drinking gin and tonics, the two of you talking with the drunken high-mindedness of fraternity boys. Later you found out from former student X that it was the real and true modus operandi of the old priest to stay up all night smoking and drinking with a former student, talking all that drunken, high-minded talk until daybreak, but then, at that moment in time when it was taking place, you thought it was the first time it had happened to either one of you. In the morning you walked the block to the beach and swam before breakfast in the gently breaking waves. He sang "O Mio Babbino Caro," plunging up and down in the easy current, and you can still see his face as it was in the early sunlight, spouting water from both nostrils and singing in Italian. Later you cooked cheese omelets then lay together side by side on the pullout sofa that was his bed, holding hands. As he drifted off to sleep his final words were not his own. They were Shake-

speare's, sort of: "I will grapple you to my bosom with hoops of
steel."

After he left you decided the whole thing had been a terrible mistake. A few months later you went to see him, in
Philadelphia, to explain it. You walked along the cobblestone
streets of Old City, sullen and intractable, refusing to hold his
hand. "Bare ruined choirs where late the sweet birds sang,"
was his reply, gazing up into the leafless branches of the maple trees.

Two lines of Shakespeare (plus a little Puccini) to fix in place
the simple but overwhelming fact: you loved another person,
even though you did your best to cancel it out or turn it into
something else, even if it was your right to cancel it out and
even if it really was something else, something other than what
you took it for at the time, whatever that was.

The ending, then: you loved him, something you were in a
big hurry to forget but which he was in a bigger hurry to remember. For he loved you also. That is the one thing you seem
most of all to avoid considering. Others he loved as well, perhaps—at least that has been your suspicion all these years,
supported mainly by the leering presence of former student
X—but he loved you, or at least the person you were in your
youth. The handsome boy with the David Bowie pants and the
nicotine-stained fingers, the frenetic teenager bursting with
promise and the will to please.

All right, love is love but resentment is also resentment, and
little by little you came to resent the way the old priest continued to look at you, as if he could fix you in a certain moment of
your life and experience and keep you there. As if you yourself
were a story to be told, and told the way he'd decided to tell it!

As if you alone could save him.

And so one day you went away, intending to return, as many another time you'd come and gone, but things happened, one thing and then the next, time and distance, and you never got the chance to go back.

You abandoned him, is what really happened.

Just face up to the ending, the real ending, even if that's not how your book ends.

The book ends with you and the old priest having martinis and Chinese takeout the evening before he is to be placed into assisted living. The book ends with the old priest, having gone a bit senile, drinking martinis and casting out imaginary demons between bites of tea-smoked duck.

But this story does not end with imaginary demons and cold dim sum.

He betrayed you, is what really happened, following which you betrayed him. You abandoned him also, following which he abandoned you.

Just face up to it. Be honest. Admit what happened and move on.

Snow behind the Door

"I MISS THAT LITTLE STREET," I SAY TO MY GRAND-
mother over coffee. "I miss that street and all those people.
I can still remember their names and what they looked
like."

We live at the seashore now, far away from the narrow
Philadelphia street where I spent my childhood and where my
grandmother lived her married life. Not long after my grandfather died she came here, to the Jersey coastal town of Limit.
"Too many memories," she told me when I came back from
Boston to find her in a different place, a different life. "I had to
go on by myself and I had to start fresh. I found a job making
beds at the Dolphin Motel. Good hard work, good girls working
there. I need the work and I need the girls, too. I made friends
here, Phil. I made a life."

Her health these last few months has taken a hard left turn,
and when I visit her she looks more puzzled than pained or
tired, as if these things were to be expected in other people.
Her right shoulder is two inches lower than her left and her
back bent sideways, crablike, when she tries to walk.

"It's like I have a cast on my shoulder and a tie rod fastened
to my back," she tells me. "At night I wake up sweating and sick.
Too many things go wrong all at once, you have to line the spe-
cialists up around the block. I go to the doctor at the corner and
he tells me, 'Old age, Rose. Old age.'"

"Cheer up," I offer. "You're doing better than many."

"Better than who, Phil, my dead relatives? And even that I'd debate."

"Take the pills," I tell her.

"It's like they make you into a zombie, those pills. Last week I took too many and by lunchtime I was sitting in a corner, talking to my aunt Alfia. The one who died in 1953." She shakes her head. "I want to be aware of whatever time I might have left."

"Take the pills, Rose. Humor me."

She takes two small blue Valium from a thin packet and washes them back with a swallow of black coffee. She smiles, her mouth closed, the upper plate removed.

"I can still see their faces," I say. "The way the light hit your door in the morning, the housefronts across the street in the afternoon."

"I've seen some of those people since, but not many and not recently. A handful of weddings and funerals." She sips her coffee. Her hair is the same shade of auburn she has dyed it for the last forty years, her watchful hazel eyes and hawk's nose, the same. The housecoat she wears is the same one she's been wearing for over twenty years, and although she is in a different house, the furnishings are the same, the dishes, the aluminum coffee pot, the family photographs that line the walls. She is lighter, though, and unless it's my imagination, maybe two inches shorter. Outside her kitchen window is no alleyway, no broken wooden fence, no stray cat or dog. High clean blue ocean sky. A tidy block of pastel bungalows by the sea.

I work an Atlantic City casino job, mid-shift. Afternoons I walk the area called the pit, back behind the table games; I watch the customers, the action. Win, loss, table inventory. People laugh,

drink, win, lose, curse, praise, live. I write. Columns of numbers, individual slips of customers who will want something
back, some return on their hard-earned cash or at least on the
risk of that hard-earned cash. Gourmet dinners, luxury suites,
champagne, limos, helicopter rides. So then I'm like a waiter,
too, a waiter in the bigtop placing orders while the crowd gasps
and the jugglers and clowns perform. Cocktail servers dressed
in the period of Louis XVI float up and down the aisles, Marie Antoinette and Pompadour hawking coffee, tea, juice. The
name of the casino is the Bastille, the irony of that name long
since lost.

Late evening I return from the noise of slot machines and bets
called out and money won and lost, the riot of desperate fun
and greed that is the casino business. I slide into bed and whisper to my wife, "I can't take it anymore. I'm at the end of my
rope."

"That's what you say every night," she sighs.

"I mean it this time, Anna. I'm at the end of something."

She pushes silently against my locked elbows. I give a few
scattered excuses, the stress and the noise, the hollow of my
chest ringing like a twenty-five-cent slot machine.

"It's all right," she tells me. "Things will improve. They'll
change."

"No they won't. I don't see where anything can go from here."

"What will you do? How will we live?"

"I don't know."

"Let's leave Limit," Anna says, stepping out of the shower. Her
tiny footprints pattern the scuffed oak hallway. She plucks
from the closet a daisy-patterned jumper, floats across the

room holding it at arm's length, the upward turn in her mood that always signals the school year's end. "We can take the equity from this house, my teacher's pension. Open a tablecloth restaurant in some small town just starting to get yuppified, gentrified, whatever they call it. Your photographs can line the walls above the tastefully upholstered banquette. I'll run the front of the house, you can cook. End of the evening you can plug in the L5, play for the people while they enjoy their espresso and tiramisu."

"Yeah, right."

"I'm serious, Phil. They have all these old industrial towns in New York State, just aching for this kind of thing. We can buy cheap, live upstairs, build the restaurant downstairs. We can start a family."

"My grandmother, just now."

"When she's better, of course."

"Well, maybe you have a point."

"I didn't marry a loser. As far as I know, anyway."

My grandmother tells stories when she gets in the mood, family stuff I've listened to since childhood and that I could recite along with her.

"Many days sitting in this house I think for no particular reason of my Uncle Cosmo," she begins, setting down the coffee cup. "And I can't think of Uncle Cosmo without thinking of his bakery on Catherine Street in Philadelphia and how one time he gave my cousin Nancy and me day-old bread to feed the sparrows that congregated there, at dusk, in the poplar trees. We fed the little birds like Easter peeps out of our hands and I can still remember the happy sounds they made in the trees and as they flew down to the pavement and all around our legs, and the entire block, for ten or fifteen minutes, seemed alive with them. In return Uncle Cosmo asked us to go to his house and tell his wife, my aunt Alfia, that he was tied up at the bakery and wouldn't be home until late that night. But when we got there my aunt Alfia—*Atsia*, in our way of calling her— told us to go back out and keep an eye on him, see if he was really in the bakery or where he might be, and report what we saw back to her.

"'Keep close to the wall,' she warned us.

"When we came back out on Catherine Street, Uncle Cosmo was closing up the shop and we hid in an alleyway across the street until we could see the shadow of his long-brimmed fedora. We followed him at a distance of half a block, keeping close to the wall as Atsia had advised us. After three more blocks he turned down Ninth Street and went into an apartment house and we could see him in the windows go up the lighted stairs. On the third floor landing he met a woman and we waited for almost an hour before we ran to tell my aunt about it and then ran back to see if he would come out and if he would come out with her or alone. There was a man standing on the street, off to the side, peeing against the wall. When he saw us girls standing there he turned his back to us. It's funny what you remember, what gets caught there. I think I'd recognize that man at a hundred yards even though I only saw him once, and for a minute, and it was dark out in that street near the market where the men were packing up their stands. It was cold but not very and the men who were not helping pack up the stands where they sold meat and cheese and produce were warming their hands by trashcan fires they made with wooden crates. They had live animals down there at that time, everything fresh, and the only thing that was on ice was the fish, big codfish and sea-bass, clams and oysters and heavy black mussels, the seaweed and barnacles still clinging to them, that my mother would buy only at the full moon: that's what she said about mussels, that they waxed and waned with the moon. She'd steam them open and then stuff them with breadcrumbs and capers and sometimes fresh garlic and basil, olive oil she'd take back from the market in a gallon jug, and she'd bake them and the smell would fill up the house we had on Wharton Street in the years before my father died."

I look up at the TV screen. Regis and Kathie Lee recommend the cruise of a lifetime. Bill Cosby communicates the raw excitement to be found inside every box of Jell-O pudding. Outside the sun falls on the clipped grass, brownish green, greenish yellow, turning with the year. We sip coffee and eat day-old poundcake.

"We're thinking of moving," I tell her, nudging time present next to time past. "I need to find another job. Plus the neighborhood's going down. All the time now, day and night, all you hear are barking dogs. I've never heard so many dogs in my life. Property values go up and the neighborhood goes down. The old islanders are dying out."

"Nothing stays the same," she agrees. "I think all the time of that house we had on Wharton Street, my father, my aunt Alfia. My Uncle Cosmo at his oven, baking bread. My age, all you do is think of the past."

"What's wrong with that?"

"I'd like to open my eyes and see right now. The older you get, the harder that is to do. Your life starts running backward on its spool."

"Those were better days."

She nods. Opens and closes the thin lids of her eyes. "Wait," she says finally. *"Ashpet."*

Early afternoon I return to the empty house; a few dogs bark, settle down as the day turns drizzly. I go up to the third floor where I have my books, a darkroom, musical equipment. The guitar is a honey-colored Gibson L5 I acquired twenty years ago—my one semester up in Boston, at Berklee—when a kid I was friendly with had the Denver Boot applied to his Alfa Romeo. I've kept it all these years, can play fifteen or twenty standards from start to finish, plus lots of twelve-bar blues lines. I like to plug the thing in once in a while and let the old dinged up Roland Jazz Chorus vibrate those bass notes down to my socks, an experience not unlike turning on a church organ and then sitting up inside the choir loft by yourself, holding onto one chord, preferably minor. I noodle on the thing, play a few riffs. But after a few minutes I set the guitar in its case, walk to the window, look down the windy street. A block of old shore homes tilted like nesting seabirds on the narrow tongue of sand that separates bay from ocean. A good northeaster and you have lobster in the living room, flounder in the foyer. Everything you worked for torn loose on the changing tide.

Thursday, my night off, I cook. Another of my interests that was once a passion, now a hobby, something to do in my "free time." Salmon in a marinade of ginger, soy, and brown sugar, spiked with Dewar's and grilled and set atop a mixture of wilted field greens: dandelion, escarole, bitter things plucked from my own backyard.

After dinner we sit out in our jackets, drink the rest of the scotch. It's a crisp, clear evening, tail end of April, and the moon is out, high and white and virginal. A sprinkling of stars northward, scent of low tide off the shallow beds of clams and oysters, south, southwest. We finish the drinks and when Anna goes in I pull the camera from the trunk of my car.

I clamp it to a tripod and attempt night photography of the flowering dogwood in the side yard. I lie on the cold ground and shoot straight up through the spiky black branches. When I move to the far end of the property and begin shooting the moon-whitened forsythia, the Chihuahua behind the fence begins to bark and then howl, yet nobody comes outside to ask why the alarm is sounding. Other dogs join in. The two mutts tied on the other side of a stand of white pines, the far corner of our property. The Rottweiler half a block away, in a pen, tethered to a pole, behind a stockade fence: Woof *woof.* Woof *woof.* Woof *woof.*

The Chihuahua on the slide-rope behind our garage: woooooooooooooooooo!

I collapse the tripod after twenty minutes and go back into the kitchen where Anna is drying dishes. She looks up at me and I answer, "Dogs."

"Oh?" she says, and tilts her head sideways, listening, birdlike.

Wooooooooooooooooooooooooo!

"You want to get rid of dogs?" a guy I work with named Harvey offers. "That's the easiest thing there is. Easy, I'm telling you, like curing a headache. You go into the gift shop and get yourself a bottle of Advil. You take a few of those pills, stuff 'em into a piece of hot dog, toss it over the fence, walk away. Good-night Lucille. Fifty pills will kill fifty dogs; they can't tolerate the Motrin. Farewell my lovely. Everything nice and quiet, I can assure you."

Coffee and Valium between trips to the doctor. High spring now and some sunshine cleft between the damp island days. She worsens in front of me, asks me to stay longer now, and always a little longer. I arrange her in the bed, wait with her the two minutes or two hours for sleep to come. Her hands always seem to be reaching for me.

"That was the month of October," she begins. "I remember because he died right after that in a sawdust fire at the RCA factory where he was a cabinetmaker, a foreman for the craftsmen who made the cabinets for Victor Talking Machines. These are a few things I remember from that time, right before the man from the factory came to tell Mom the news. I remember that man peeing while we watched Uncle Cosmo go into that house and then up the lighted stairs and then later we walked down the block and past the market and stood outside the house where my uncle and aunt lived and there was a big fight and we could hear him yelling in his broken English, 'Some damma girls. You believe some little damma girls make up stories. Whata house? Whata stairs? Whata woman?' I remember the wooden stalls set up halfway into the street, the smell of mussels baked with capers and olive oil and breadcrumbs, the way that man looked on the pavement as he turned his back to us.

"Another time Pop brought home a sack of oysters and he sat on this wooden bench in the kitchen shucking them, and he put out sliced lemons and some catsup. I can still taste the seawater as it rolled out of the shell onto my tongue, and I've never tasted anything as wonderful again. That's the last time I can remember Pop eating with us, and my brother Jack was late coming in—he used to play pinochle with some friends of his in a room back behind Goldstein's Funeral Parlor—and Pop threw a fit about it, his lateness that is, not the fact that he'd been playing pinochle in a mortuary. He turned the table with the oysters and all the condiments over in front of Jack and Jack told Pop that it was his dinner and he could do whatever he liked with it, he wasn't spiting anybody but himself. That made Pop even madder and he threw Jack out that night. I remember Mom crying over it and all the oysters in their shells scattered on the brick floor of the kitchen and Mom sweeping them up with a straw broom. That was the last time Jack saw my father, and he always talked about it afterward. A week later they came, two men I think it was now, from the RCA factory in Camden and gave Mom the news. She couldn't understand all of it because of her English but in a little while I came home from the movies, it was a Saturday and I had gone to see *The Phantom of the Opera* with my cousins, and I came into the house and the man told me and I had to tell Mom in Italian what he was saying and he had a check and she had to sign a paper right then to get it. She signed and I was crying and everybody as they came in and it got closer to dinner found out and they were crying except for my brother Jack, who wasn't there because Pop had thrown him out.

"I had a brother Joe, too, who wasn't living with us because he was a deaf mute and hard to control. Some relatives in Atlantic City were taking care of him for us because they had no children and we were nine, counting Babe who my mother was pregnant with on that day the two men came with the news and the paper to sign. After the money ran out and we couldn't give the family in Atlantic City anything toward keeping Joe they sent him back to us. He was about sixteen and he worked laying mosaics in a church they were building. He didn't want to come back with us and he didn't want to leave his job making beautiful pictures of saints and angels and he didn't want to go away from the ocean. These things he told me in sign language. Then when he found out Pop was dead we couldn't control him. I was the only one who could understand him even a little. We had French doors in that house, one in every doorway of every room and Joe lost his temper and kept trying to tell us something and I remember everyone asking me, What's he saying? What's he saying? He broke every window in the house that night and finally the police came and took him away and we never saw him again.

"*Noviembre misi ri muorti, 'rarrieri a puorta a nivi*, my mother said when he was gone, and crossed herself and went into her bedroom to light three candles, because the following day was All Souls'. November, month of the dead, snow behind the door."

Later, an early dinner. Too much wine, too much thinking, I call out sick from the job. I fall asleep with the TV on, dream of a place with silver-black borders that pulse and quiver. There are men walking in a line, a train, scenes of battle. Violence, well anticipated, welcome. Deep in the night I wake up, middle of May already, screens in the open windows. Silty bay rot of clams and oysters, fog pushing in on the changing tide. A dog barks, long and shrill; another dog joins in, then two more.

Woof *woof.* Woof *woof.* Woof *woof.*

"These dogs," Anna says, turning out of sleep. "I can't remember a time when dogs didn't bark. Did you say something to me just now? I dreamed I was alone in a room. There was a white wall and on the other side of the wall a man was praying. What do you think that means?"

Why does it have to mean anything?

"I dreamed," I say, turning on my back and telling her a dream, only not the one I've just had. "It was fall, wind and leaves. There was a schoolgirl standing under a streetlight watching a man pee against the side of a brick storefront."

"Were you the man or the girl?"

"I don't know." I pull her close up in the bed, her tiny bird's shoulders, the warm, creased narrow of her back. "I don't know if I was anybody."

Red dice luft, fall, skitter on green felt.

"What's up with you?" Harvey asks.

"My grandmother's been sick. I don't sleep at night. Those dogs," I say. "The dogs I was telling you about? Driving me crazy. Just absolutely over the top. Just one dog, really, that starts the rest of them off."

"I told you what I'd do."

"I might even be desperate enough to consider it, but here's the problem. I looked over the fence the other night. There's a bad dog and there's a good dog. The good dog is a basset hound, or something like that. You never hear it. Through the gaps in the fence I can see the little legs moving, but that's it. If I put the hot dog in there, suppose the good dog eats it?"

"Toss in six or seven pieces," Harvey advises. "That should be enough for them both." Harvey looks out into the dark crowded aisle, the crowd swarming beneath the crabbed glare of neon and stale cigarette smoke. "Let the aisles flow with the blood of the innocent and the guilty alike!"

I stand at the fence, the suit still on my back, the tie at half-mast around my neck. The moon sits on the housetops, yellow and full and low.

"Your dog," I explain to the neighbor lady. "The little one, there. He barks frequently, disturbs me, my wife. Disturbs the other dogs, for that matter." I smile, try to be polite, off-handed. "You'll have to make an effort to control him. Please."

"Why?"

"Because it's the responsible thing to do. It's the law, anyway."

"Do I even *know* you?"

"No, but I live here. Plenty of people around here you don't know, I don't know them either. It doesn't have anything to do with what we're talking about here."

"And what is it we're talking about here, stranger?"

"Common decency."

She twists her mouth up, like snapping a change purse shut.

"I need peace," I confess. "My grandmother, she's not well."

"Does your grandmother live in that house with you?"

"No."

We stare at one another.

"It's a dog," she says, and stares through me, a yellow moon dancing in each black eye. "It barks. *Bow-wow*," she says, and walks away as if that's all anybody would need to know about it. She turns, framed by the light cast down inside her open doorway.

The police, I'm about to say. *I'll involve the police.*

She flops one pointed breast out of the strapless sundress and wiggles it in my direction. "Who says I'm decent, or want to be?" she asks, calling down the short length of dog-rutted turf. Greatly amused.

Early summer and the patch of garden by the back door planted and staked. My grandmother slides, cancer of the pancreas, inoperable. She's in a hospital bed, breathing through a tube. The rotted pit of her mouth flung open, gasping air. Hawk's nose, auburn hair running white from the scalp. Asleep in the arms of Demerol.

I stand staring at a row of blackjack tables as absently as you watch water flowing. To my right a young couple. The kid plays badly and the girl worse than that. Every time the girl decides something that results in a losing hand the kid laughs at her, calls her an idiot, an imbecile, a cute little moron.

It's like the Indian thing, I tell myself, staring at the cartoon characters who mob the aisles. *Maya*, the world of illusion.

Finally I say to the blonde, "Have you been dating him long?"

The blonde looks puzzled, uncertain.

"This man you're sitting next to. How long have you been dating him?"

"Two years," she says, smiling. Flashes the ring. "We're engaged to be married, October the ninth one year."

"You should be careful," I advise. "Be careful how you choose."

"Is this, like, some stupid joke," the kid says, looking up from his hand of cards. "Is there, like, a hidden camera, filming this?"

"No joke," I tell the kid. "Far from funny." I glance down at my own spreading middle with the resentment of a man who'd expected the awkward thinness of adolescence to become the graceful thinness of middle age. Instead, it has been replaced by an equally awkward corpulence.

"I can have your job for this," the kid threatens.

"Take my job. Please. See, *that's* a joke."

"Get me your supervisor," the kid says, stammering. "I want to talk to the pit boss."

"I am the pit boss," I inform the stupid kid. To the blonde I say, "You should be careful how you choose. It's important. You think it's not? Just take a good look at me if you don't believe it."

On the shuttle that takes us back to our cars Harvey says, "I had this job, one time, when I was in high school. Carting dead dogs out to a place in the woods. The shelter I worked for was killing them, then I'd take them away. Back then the doctor did them with a needle right into the heart. You'd watch them stiffen for a second, then go soft. I always remember how limp the bodies were, still warm, you'd see the fleas still clinging to them. I'd open the tailgate and jump in there, right in the middle of the pile. Just start tossing them into the pit. Then I'd throw a couple of bags of lime over them and pick the shovel up."

He laughs, stands up in the aisle when the bus comes to a rocking halt.

"It was illegal dumping, Phil. I was making more than any other kid in my high school and buying my girlfriend gold better than what her mother was wearing. When she found out what I was doing, though, she ditched me. People are a fucked up bunch of people," he observes. "I keep living my life and watching them live theirs and I keep coming up with the same sorry conclusion."

Thursday, another night off, more *free time.*

Home from the hospital we open wine, start a late supper. The trumpet of Miles Davis fills the house, breathes in and out the curtainless windows, pencil-thin, bone-bare. "On Green Dolphin Street."

"I'll do it," offers Anna. "You relax. Sit in the yard. Have another glass of wine. Try to rest. They said they'd call. And I'll call the rest of your family. They've been leaving messages on the machine all week. Just sit down for a bit. Just try and relax."

I slump down with a glass of Chardonnay under the drooping branches of an overgrown holly tree. The Chihuahua barks, settles in, barks again. The basset hound follows, out of character. A shrill bark, two deep barks, then other dogs in other yards join in. The Rottweiler on the next block over: Woof *woof.* Woof *woof.*

"How do you do it?" I asked Harvey. "Tell me again."

"You snip the end off a hot dog and cut a small slit in it and into that slit you insert two or three pills. You say, 'Here, little fella. Take two of these and call me in the morning, little goodfella. Woof woof.' That's how you do it."

Behind the stockade fence doglegs slant and flicker. I've prepared one piece only and my intention is to fling it over the fence, carefully, at the little dog's feet. Try my luck, hope for silence. But just as I'm ready a low-flying bug sails into the arc of my own porchlight, lands on my own lawn chair. A praying mantis, I observe it close up: the round unblinking headlights of its eyes; the hooked mandible, precise and elegant. The mantis sits upright on the slippery Grosfillex, cocks its back leg forward and grooms the splintered stick of its own body, dog-like. I nod; the insect tips its armored head sideways. Bluejays screech and rustle in the holly branches overhead. A telephone rings. Dogs bark. A door creaks open. The neighbor lady stands alone on her back step, waving and smiling frantically. "Hi neighbor!" she cries out. "Hello, neighbor, hello!" She calls the dogs into the house in the exaggerated style of a movie farmer calling pigs. "Here, dogs, *dogs dogs dogs! Heeere*, dogs!" She gathers the Chihuahua up into her arms, instructs the snuffling basset to hurry up. Kicks the door closed with a flourish behind her. I stand for a moment in the backwash of silence. The space of light above her door blinks into darkness. I touch my closed fist to the side of the lawn chair and the praying mantis floats up into darkness. "Come back," I say, but in front of me only the evidence of this day and time of day: a dozen Gypsy moths twisting in the porchlight as if looped on sewing thread, the flowering tomato vines by the back steps staked and tied with ribboned bedsheets, Anna's shadow expanding and contracting just inside the backlit door space. Behind the screen the scent of dinner.

Some memories of early childhood: a powder blue Fairlane with a white convertible top and white sidewall tires; a trip to the Pocono Mountains, a little lopsided cabin in a tangle of trees; a trip to the seashore, tiny blue swimfins and a green scuba mask; an unpleasant scene in the Melrose Diner; a car accident on Christmas Eve, after which I came to live with my grandmother and grandfather, working people who never lost the disquieted look of those who become parents for the first time late in life.

The City of Gold

COUPLES DO DIFFERENT THINGS WHEN they're about to break up. Charlie and I fly to New Mexico. We spend the afternoon in the lounge of the Albuquerque Hilton, drinking margaritas and listening to a flamenco guitarist. They don't proof me. I look older, I've always looked older. Charlie tells me I was *born* older.

"I can come out here and get a leg up," Charlie says, licking salt from the rim of his glass. "If I'm going to work in the casino business then I should make as much money as I can." He's got on a lime-green golf shirt and tan chinos, and his thinning blond hair is clipped straight across the forehead, like Caesar, maybe, but a little *boy* Caesar, which makes me melt for him when I think about it. Charlie can still do that: he can still cause me unexpectedly to melt.

"That's true," I say, ruffling his bangs with my little finger. "Time is money, baby. Tick tick tick."

Charlie's friend Rodman is helping with the startup of Indian gaming in New Mexico. The Indians are working on a compact with the state to expand their bingo halls into full-fledged casinos and Rodman called Charlie up to say that there is money to be made, fun to be had. He wants to put a few people he can trust around him while he jockeys for position.

"I've got to take this, I think," Charlie says, stroking my hair,

tugging the silver buckle at my throat. "I've got to start thinking about the future, Amber. What about you?"

After the drinks we drive into Old Town, buzzed on mescal, en-
ergetic and trippy. The streets have this hushed quality, as if it's
one of the unspoken rules of the place that you shouldn't be in a
hurry. The buildings are old, stately, with historical plaques on
the doors and fence posts. There are a lot of people who look
like Asians walking around and I decide they're the Indians,
the Native Americans of New Mexico. The white guys you see
have long hair and wear bell-bottomed jeans and the girls wear
denim skirts and blouses overflowing with embroidery, and
I've never considered that a different part of the United States
could really be, well, so different. New Mexico, we learn in one
of the brochures I've picked up at the front desk, was settled
by the conquistadors who came up from Central America on
rumors of the lost city of gold, El Dorado.
    "Gaily bedight," Charlie says.
    "Huh?"
    "It's Poe, from a poem called 'Eldorado.' A knight sets out to
find gold but finds death instead."
    Charlie was an English major in college, about a hundred
years ago, and is always throwing that stuff around, famous
lines from literature and film, and I like that, I mean, I always
thought I'd be with a guy who had some education, but then
again he hasn't really done anything with it, either. He often
complains he can't figure out what he wants to be when he
grows up. Myself, I'm still in school. I'm nineteen years old, actually. I've been with Charlie since I was sixteen. Some people
have an issue with that, but I know Charlie's always done what's

best for me. In fact, I'm sure that if it doesn't work out I'll never again have a man treat me as well as Charlie has.

"I can take the shift boss job," Charlie explains, "and you can transfer to the University of New Mexico. This could definitely be cool."

He pulls me by the hand down the winding leafy streets of Old Town, *ristras* on the painted doors and in the windows and hanging down from the spindle-posted galleries, dried red peppers everywhere you look. At the Museum of Natural History we watch a movie about the Anasazi, "the people." Their civilization flourished for centuries, then disappeared without a trace. The film shows naked, primitive people jumping around in a stream, their faces covered with mud. Then in the next scene it's night and they're in a cave, huddled in their animal skins around a brightly burning fire.

"Just vanished," Charlie says at the refreshment stand, and he makes his fingertips go *poof* as if he right then and there might suddenly vanish into thin air. "A few petroglyphs, a bunch of caves heaped with broken pottery and animal bones. And that's it, babycakes; that's all she wrote on *that* piece of rock."

"I want to get married, start a family," Charlie says to me deep in the night. He is up over me, huge in the silver light that seeps in around the edges of the drapery. "Do yourself a favor and wise up."

"I'm trying to get wise, Charlie," I say, fitting myself against him. "I really am."

Charlie was married once, before I met him, to a girl named Tina. He's got pictures of her doing all his friends. He's even got a picture of her doing his German Shepherd—only a handjob, but even so. That was in the go-go eighties, all the cocaine and depravity: in the end he just sat back and took Polaroids. With me he liked to brag that he'd gotten a good one and trained her right. And my mom, June, was liberal enough about it; she knew I'd only sneak around anyway. Sometimes she'd come over to our apartment and Charlie would make Old Fashioneds, which is her favorite drink. June always drank too much and got weepy and asked Charlie how he was treating her little girl.

"Good, as far as I know," Charlie would say, throwing a protective arm around my shoulder. And it was true: he sent me to college, bought me clothes, anything I wanted. I've never worked a job in my life except for the year before I met Charlie when I was waitressing weekends at the Portland Café in Ventnor, which is downbeach from Atlantic City. Charlie was living up the street, coming in for breakfast and then catching the jitney to work, a big friendly guy in Armani, a casino pit boss who tipped five dollars for a five-dollar breakfast.

It wasn't long before he had me in his power.

For the first few weeks I'd go over to his place after school and we'd just kiss. I'd get all heated up and then he'd send me home. Some nights we'd sit drinking with his friends at this lopsided picnic table in the kitchen. They were all younger casino people who rented rooms from Charlie in the ramshackle shore house *he* rented from an old lady who had been friendly with his mother and who now lived in Jupiter Beach, Florida. Charlie and his friend Stan the drunken plumber had their names on the lease and sublet rooms by the month, sometimes even by the week. Stan tinkered with the utility meters. It was like a big, goofy commune, with Charlie as the leader. All the girls who lived there were after Charlie, but it was me he chose. He brought me up to sit by him at the table one night and put his arm around me and that was that. As soon as we slept together he told me to quit the luncheonette and concentrate on my schoolwork. Sometimes, late at night, he liked to do my hair. He'd pick out my clothes, ask me about my friends, nodding approval or disapproval at what I told him. I thought he was a weirdo but I kept going back for more, I wasn't sure why except that I felt safe with him. At the same time the sex started getting rougher. He'd try things, whisper in my ear, "Is it good? Do you like that?" The spankings got harder, then he used a stick or a straightened coat hanger. And I wore all the plaid skirts, the English schoolgirl outfits he picked out for me. My friends laughed, but I didn't care. It turned me on that I was turning him on, my little plaid skirt and white stockings, the patent leather Mary Janes and the Coach dog collar and my dimpled, upturned bum.

Next morning we have breakfast in the room and then drive out to Rodman's casino, the Florecita Gaming Palace, which is in the desert twenty miles south of Albuquerque, just off the Interstate. It's low and long and white, like an oversized igloo, with turquoise and gold and tangerine patterns screaming off the stuccoed sides of it. On the wall next to the main door is an oversized wooden sign that says NO CAMERAS and then in smaller print gives all the penalties for bringing cameras anywhere near an Indian reservation.

"Why do you think that is?" I ask Charlie.

"They think cameras steal your soul. That your image is a part of you and if somebody takes it they take a part of you."

"Oh." I don't know what else to say. Can they be serious?

Inside the place is quiet, a few coins trickling like bright water through the slot machines. At the far end a bingo game is in progress, a row of Indian ladies sitting with their cards spread out in front of them like all the fat, tired ladies sitting at every bingo game in the history of the world. To the left you go up a few steps to a room with a snack bar, about eight blackjack tables, a roulette wheel, and a craps table. It looks like something they'd rig back East for a fundraiser at a Catholic grammar school.

"This is your leg up?" I say.

"Don't be so fast," Charlie says. He goes up to a small, dried-out woman with beige hair at a podium next to the snack bar and asks for Rodman who, as it turns out, is in a meeting. Charlie plays five-dollar blackjack to pass the time.

"If they don't believe in cameras, what do they do about surveillance?" I ask. "I never heard of a casino yet that didn't have cameras in the ceiling."

"They're Indians," he says, pointing at the smoky glass bubble above our blackjack table. "But they know like everybody else not to let their beliefs stand in the way of making a buck. Even making some dough. Get it? Buck, doe, Indians! Get it?"

"Yeesh!"

There are a few people in flannel shirts and jeans milling around the games. The dealers root for the players and remark on players' hands and what they should do and, from Charlie's standpoint, the whole thing is very unprofessional. He gets up from one table after the dealer has apologized three times for taking his money.

"It's your job," Charlie tells him, picking up his chips and moving to a seat at the next table. We've been here less than thirty minutes and already Charlie is chasing his money while I sit in a chair backed out into the aisle, watching him. The dealer stares at me, deals another hand, looks some more, smiles. His face is tight and shiny, all lines and angles, topped off with kinky blond hair that appears to be preserved under about ten coats of Afro Sheen. He's muscular in a stringy, pulled-out sort of way, and you can see the hard contours of his body shift and move underneath the turquoise and purple dealer's shirt, which is open at the throat. A golden head of Jesus tilts and bobs in the hollow beneath his Adam's apple: suffering face; barbed, bloody crown of thorns.

"Well, well," he says, slapping down the cards. "Pret-ty, pret-ty la-dy." His eyes go flooey in their sockets. He smiles a set of long, skinny teeth that look as if they've been set in plaster of Paris. "You know her?" he says to Charlie. "She bothering you?"

"She's been following me around," Charlie tells him and laughs his amused, above-it-all Charlie laugh. "I can't seem to shake her."

"She ask you for money?"

"All day long."

The blackjack dealer runs his tongue quickly over the ends of his teeth. Charlie is laughing but not turning around to see if I'm laughing too.

"I'll call security," the blackjack dealer says. The nameplate on the front of his shirt says "Maurice Baltimore." He turns to get the attention of the supervisor standing directly behind him.

Charlie says, "I was kidding. Oh gosh, you're not serious."

"That's one seriously pretty lady," he says.

"Deal the cards," Charlie says. But Maurice Baltimore stands there as if he's decided to take a break. He looks at me until I look away. He's staring at my face, my breasts, my bare legs crossed beneath the short plaid skirt.

"So she is with you?"

"Sure," Charlie says. "What did you think?"

"I don't know what to think," Maurice says. "I only know what people tell me. So she is with you."

"Of course she is."

"How much you want for her?"

Charlie turns around in his chair without saying anything. He looks at *me*.

"I'm with him and we're here to see his friend Mister *Rod*-man," I say, and glare back at him.

"Oh well then." But he keeps staring at me, eyes blue as a China plate, slapping the cards down in short precise strokes and smiling the entire time, or something that is like a smile, his mouth rearranging itself moment by moment, his expressions changing like a video run at fast-forward. "You folks from around here?"

"I'm here to see my friend Rodman about a job," Charlie says. "We're from Atlantic City."

"Rodman is cool," Maurice Baltimore says. "You a friend of Rodman then you must be cool, too."

"I am," Charlie says, and puts down a bet for him in the spot next to his own money.

"The green stuff is very cool."

"How long've you been doing this?" Charlie asks.

"Man, I been out here about nearly three or four months," Maurice Baltimore explains. He stops at the end of the hand and starts talking to Charlie as if there isn't a game to deal or other people who are waiting for their cards. "I hed a dream," he tells Charlie. "I was working in this crab house. Man, you get to smell of the job. Cooking crabs all day long in the Innermotherlovingharbor. That was me, and one day a little voice said, 'You have some Old Bay, Mo, how about some New Bay?' So I hed a dream, and in this dream the voice told me to pack up my car and drive to New Mexico. Two days nonstop, baby, and that was one hell of a ride. I came out here to this place and the man said, 'Can you deal blackjack?' And I said, 'No I can't, but I can if you show me how!' They were so desperate for people to run these games they took me off the street and put me right to work. It's an amazing phenomenon how a body gets around in this world. But one thing I say and that is, if you hear voices then you better either listen to them or go see a doctor."

The other players laugh, four dark-skinned guys who look like Indians, or Mexicans, or some combination of the two. Baltimore is white, seems white: tight blond Afro, sandy-colored mustache and chin whiskers. Only his speech and mannerisms are black, in an exaggerated way, as if he might be putting us on, but who knows?

He deals another hand, pointing the cards downward, his long fingers decorated in turquoise and silver. "Joints are doing well," he tells Charlie, "but the state is trying to close us down."

"Is that right?" Charlie asks. He knows very well that the Indians don't have a compact in place. That's the trouble with moving out here: the job could disappear in a year or two.

"The state doesn't want us to have it," the guy sitting next to Charlie says. "The state says it would be bad for the people and their image. What does the state know? It's all about the white man keeping the red man down, the same worn tune."

"Amen to that," Maurice says.

The guy looks at Charlie and says, "Not you, I mean, but you know, the government."

"I know I know," Charlie says, "I'm totally sympathetic. I have friends who work for the Indians in Connecticut. They're only about a sixteenth Indian and pay not one penny of federal income tax. I mean, they don't even *look* like Indians."

"Man is sympathetic," Maurice says. "Man is overspilling with the milk of human sympathy."

"Actually," Charlie says, "it's funny: they look like black people."

"What's funny about that?" Maurice wants to know. "What exactly is funny about looking like a black person?"

"Nothing," Charlie says, "except it's funny if you're supposed to be an Indian."

"Maybe I'm an Indian," Maurice says. "Maybe that's why that voice told me to come out here to live in the desert. Otherwise, I wouldn't be able to tell you why. I mean, I like it here but, you know, there's no trees. I miss the green is what I'm trying to say. I've got to see some green!"

Charlie takes the hint, places a bet for him, says, "Here's some green for you," then loses that hand and five more.

"No luck today," Maurice says when Charlie finally stands up. "Bye-bye, pretty lady," he says to me, and winks, and points his finger like firing a toy gun. "Come back when you can stay awhile."

Charlie goes over to the desk to see if Rodman is available, but the woman we talked to earlier says he's still in a meeting. She's got a smoker's lined face and is wearing a cheap tan suit, pilled at the elbows and hips. "He'll be sorry he missed you," she says. "Why don't you have some lunch on us?"

"We're going out to see some sights," Charlie tells her. "I'll call him later."

When we get outside the noontime heat hits me like my knees are going to buckle.

"That place is strictly amateur night," Charlie says. "I can't believe I'm stuck two hundred dollars on a chickenshit game like that."

We've rented a fire-engine-red Mustang with a white convertible top. It's April now, chill and melty back East; here it's warm and dry and you can see snow on the peaks of the mountains north of here, up toward Santa Fe. We ride with the top down and I feel good again. I put the whole weird episode with Maurice Baltimore behind me. There's no figuring Charlie sometimes. I mean, you could argue that he felt the whole thing was beneath him. After all, what competition, what threat from some lunatic dealing blackjack out in the middle of the desert? I go to move closer to him but the stick shift is in the way. We drive the highway up into the hills.

"I want to go over to this pueblo where they're having a special feast day," I tell Charlie. "It's one of only two days a year when outsiders are invited." He studies the map in the guidebook when we pull over at a high cliff that overlooks a little brown valley with boxy yellow houses scattered over it. The guidebook says that "pueblo" is a synonym for tribe, for the physical space that the tribe occupies, or for an individual in a tribe. The guidebook explains: "The people and where they live and their identity as individuals are not distinguishable, one from the other."

The San Ysidro Pueblo is farther up in the hills. The fields and open spaces shimmer in the heat, the dip and curve of the sparse rocky landscape that leads to a place where the San

Ysidro Indians have been living for centuries. Cars are parked every which way, older-make American models with dull paint jobs and dinged fenders and mangy blistered vinyl tops. Charlie pulls the Mustang beside a shallow ditch. A line of people is moving steadily in one direction; we fall in line and get moved along with them. On the left side of the dirt road are trailers with TV antennas bending from the roofs like dead trees, and the sides of the trailers are patched with scraps of sheet metal and painted different mismatched colors.

"Like another country," Charlie says. "Strictly Third World."

"It's how they live," I say.

We walk up about fifty yards, then down into a little gorge, people everywhere, Indians and also some white people wearing Western clothes. The Indians, too, wear cowboy hats, some of them. It seems that every man but Charlie is wearing boots. There is a sound of chanting and beating drums that gets louder as we walk along. Finally we stop at a place so crowded we can barely raise our arms. A gigantic stag's head is hanging from the peak of a barn at the far end of an open field, antlers tipped against the desert's electric-blue sky, the dancing men lined up on either side draped in animal skins, their faces painted with dark, scary colors. On the opposite side of the field is a pile of wood, dried branches and also scraps of lumber, wooden crates, all this wood heaped up to make a bonfire, which, the guidebook tells us, will be lit exactly at sunset. Off to the side of that, and a little behind it, is a gigantic wooden cross made of two railroad ties fastened with heavy braided rope.

"Elk's head," Charlie says, and I turn back toward the other side of the field. "Look at the goddamn size of it." The man next to him shuffles his feet and spits on the ground. Charlie keeps staring at the dancers. "They dance all day," he says. "It's their ritual. I feel like we've barged in on something sacred."

"They invited us," I say.

"We should go," Charlie says. "We should leave these people to their own lives."

"I'd like to stay for the bonfire," I say, but Charlie moves on without answering me.

Just ahead an old woman sits on the cinderblock steps of her trailer, tossing dried corn to a gathering of small black birds. Two mongrel dogs scrabble in the dust, bony animals with mangy ruffs like the last part of the old wolf strain. They jimmy up on their hind legs to snarl and fight. The old woman stands to kick them free of one another, and the children playing in the dirt laugh at the sight of it. There are makeshift wooden stands lined up between the trailers and shacks and the place smells of dust and animals and meat cooking in large black pots and sizzling on rusted hibachis. Charlie buys us two wooden skewers with chunks of blackened meat clinging to them like stringy tendons.

"What is this?" Charlie asks after he's already paid for it.

"Meat on a stick," the old man behind the stand tells us.

"What kind?"

"All kinds. Put some lead in your pencil, kemosabe."

The meat is tough and has a sour taste of urine.

"Good?" the man says.

"Good," Charlie says.

"That's meat to make warriors and husbands strong and women to love their men in the secret place where we come to our bodies and then for a small while at least are free of them."

"You said it!" Charlie laughs.

We walk away from the greasy old man, his iron-colored hair in fat braids across his chest.

"This meat is making me sick," Charlie says. He throws the half-eaten stick of meat into a trashcan fire where two girls stand huddled, dropping little paper dolls and wooden objects from an old-fashioned cigar box. They stop what they're doing and look at Charlie.

"Now we have to start all over again," one of the girls whines.

"Sorry," Charlie says.

"That's all right," she tells Charlie with a shrug. "You don't know any better."

"This is no place for tourists," Charlie says, and starts walking back toward the car. "This is just abject poverty on display."

Back in the room Charlie snaps the leash on the dog collar, says giddyap, and then apologizes for mixing his metaphors. He goes on for a long time. It's what I want, it's what I think I want. Only it doesn't do anything for me. Maybe once, but no more. He does everything right, only nothing gets exchanged; we stay in our own two separate compartments. He keeps asking me if it's good. I want it to be good, only it's not. It's *boring.* How much longer can I wait? But while it's going on I think of the strange guy in the casino this morning. I think of Maurice Baltimore, the way he looked at me. A guy like that, he'd be capable of anything, I guess. I feel his eyes on me still. It was like he was raping me and Charlie was laughing and handing him money for his trouble. I close my eyes and keep them shut. I think of New Mexico, dry riverbeds and strange languages, men who are used to finding themselves in desperate situations, places with stories that always start out, "She was last seen—" I imagine Charlie in a room with me and in walks Maurice Baltimore. "I want the girl. The girl is mine now," says Maurice. He goes to grab me by the wrist but Charlie takes out a pistol and shoots him dead on the spot, burns him right down. I want to be won back and Charlie wins me back.

Toward the end of last winter I moved back home. I couldn't admit it to June, of course, but the reason I left is that I found Charlie with a girl in our apartment, some kid he picked up in the casino, some ponytailed little Vietnamese—tiny hips, tiny arms, tiny sprout of hair between her tiny legs—looking up from where she knelt on the floor, my patchwork quilt spread out under her in the chilly afternoon.

Later, when Charlie finally caught up with me, he explained that it was a once in a while thing, a "peccadillo," as he called it, something he'd picked up in the service for Chrissakes: he thought I was a more adventurous person than that. I moved back in with June, started seeing guys my own age. They liked the plaid skirts and they liked the dog collar. They liked my up-turned bum, too. A few times Charlie called and June told him I was out, she never knew when she might see me, she couldn't control me.

"June," Charlie pleaded while I listened in on the extension, "talk some sense to that daughter of yours. Her priorities are all screwed up."

And June did try to talk sense to me. "I must say he's treated you well," June offered late one night, a library copy of *Glitz* fallen open on her lap. "Are you sure you know what you're doing?"

"Whose mother are you?" is what I wanted to know.

"You can stay here for a while," June said, stifling a yawn, "but then you'll have to get a job and do something for your-self for a change." She looked at me over the tops of two tortoise-shell half-moons and added, "And I don't want Mr. S disturbed. He lives here too, you know."

Mr. S is Sam Santora, a sleazy old guido who runs an escort service, a guy who, if he had to choose between his midnight-blue Lincoln Town Car and the starving millions of Africa, he would choose the Town Car, every time, *fuhgettaboudit*. I came back home to find June with her library books and her Old Fashioneds, her Mr. S and her decorator house in Margate, ev-erything arranged just so.

"Amber's visiting for a spell," she told Mr. S. "Amber's be-tween engagements."

"Let me know if you want to go to work," said Mr. S. "Those outfits of yours will go over big with my customers."

"Mr. S!" shrieked June.

"I'm just trying to help the kid out. If she don't want my help then all she's gotta do is say so."

"I don't want your help, Sam."

"See there, she don't want my help. She'd rather give it away."

June only stamped her feet and said, "Mr. S, if you say an-other word—well, I just don't know what!"

The other casino is high up on a bare, pitted hill. Charlie says he wants to win back his two hundred, which is *so* Charlie, hedge if you're winning and send it in on the downturn. The place is the same size as Rodman's casino but completely different inside. The games move fast, the way they do back East, and the lights are low, everything crowded together on a black rug with squiggles of red, yellow, and blue running through it like party streamers. The dealers wear the same pattern on their vests and bow ties.

"How appropriate," Charlie says. "The employees match the carpet."

The cocktail servers are also dressed in matching Spandex catsuits, and you can get soda or juice but no alcohol because it's an Indian reservation. In New Mexico, we learn in the guidebook, it's still on the books that a bartender can't serve an Indian a drink. We walk the casino floor a full circle, then Charlie leaves without making a bet. He says he'd rather not throw good money after bad.

Instead, we stop at a place down the road—the area's best, according to the guidebook—a fancy room with wide pine vigas and a clay fireplace, flamenco music wafting. We drink margaritas made with Cuervo 1800 and Grand Marnier, eight dollars apiece; the menu features Southwestern specialties like wood-grilled saddle of elk and pan-seared rattlesnake.

"That's like something sacred we witnessed," Charlie says, explaining the festival to me the way he always explains everything. "Or what's left of it anyway. Something that's lost to us, but I guess it's lost to them too. Little torn up bits of Native American religion and Christianity fastened together with duct tape."

The waitress says, "You folks from around here?"

"That seems to be the question of the day."

"Well, you stand out just a *bit.*"

"We're in the casino business," Charlie tells her. "What do you think of Indian gaming in New Mexico, if you don't mind my asking?"

"I think they're like little children and they need to be protected," the waitress answers without missing a beat. She's got blond hair and shocking cat-green eyes. "I've lived out here since I was five. Bingo has been disaster enough. They say the casinos are for the tourists, but the people who'll get hurt by it are the Indians themselves. They'll drink till they drop and would rather bet every last penny in their pocket, sell their car and then walk home. Anything the white man introduces only brings more trouble."

"Well," Charlie says, "I did ask."

"Another round!" I holler, slamming my fist down on the heavy wooden table.

The waitress smiles knowingly at me and pirouettes away.

Charlie sips his drink and talks his big talk; I've heard it all before. First we were going to have an upscale deli. Then we were going into the charter fishing business. Then it was a life insurance pyramid scheme. In his mind Charlie goes from this to that. "Could you live in a place like this?" he wants to know. "We could get a real house. I'm tired of living in other people's houses. And I'm not the only one who's not getting any younger, Amber."

"I'm nineteen," I say. "Speak for yourself."

"You were sixteen years old and one hundred two pounds and you were beautiful," Charlie says in his best Rod Steiger. He takes my face in his oversized hands and in his eyes I see sadness, for the first time I think, and that he's getting tired, shocking to see, the old sport is getting played out. "Can't you," he whines. "Can't you just—"

"What?" I say. "What, Charlie? What?"

But he only looks at me and shakes his head.

The best time for us was when Charlie had that house on Portland Avenue, the gang of us sitting up drinking all night at that picnic table in Charlie's kitchen. I liked to cut school and hang around the place in the afternoons when everybody was at their jobs. I'd clean the house, think about what I would fix for dinner. Stan the drunken plumber was always coming on to me when Charlie wasn't around. Then one day he cornered me on my way out of the bathroom. He forced himself on me without bothering to find out if he had to. When it was over I gathered up my clothes and said, "I'm going to tell Charlie about this, you know."

"No, you won't," Stan said. "And we both know why you won't."

And I never did, although I'm still not sure what Stan meant by that. But not even a week later the old lady who owned the house was back in New Jersey for a funeral, dropped in for a peek one morning and had a nervous breakdown. She said she'd trusted Charlie: now look at her lovely house in squalor. The authorities padlocked the front door and Charlie and I found an apartment together. June helped me box up my things, then took me out for a fifty-dollar lunch followed by an afternoon at the Lady Day Spa.

Rodman is tall and swarthy, he wears Italian suits, you notice his teeth. Two years ago he beat skin cancer: melanoma on his face from twenty years of surfing days and working nights. When the doctor told him he was clear he said his life was changed; he signed up for karate lessons, went to night college, learned to play the saxophone. He packed up his wife and three kids and moved to Albuquerque.

"This is a big day for the pueblos out here," Rodman says. "We've decided to turn it into an employee appreciation day." We're standing in the middle of a bingo hall decorated with ribbons and piñatas; there is a buffet table and a band playing loud music on a low stage, like a homemade wedding reception. Maurice Baltimore is the lead singer. He's got his purple dealer's shirt on, a black sports jacket draped over it. He's sweating and screaming into the mic.

"McSween has got the whole thing locked with Abraham Two Bears," Rodman explains over the noise. "You remember McSween? He was lucky if he could pay a six dollar six. Forget I just said that. Now he gets two percent of the drop, right off the top, two goddamn percent."

"Strong," Charlie says.

"You'd have your own shift, Charlie, and report directly to me. It's a piece of cake. Just leave the Indian chicks alone— sorry, Amber—and if somebody gets undesirable, you can eject them like a shot. The guards carry pieces. I mean, this is Federal. You don't get out of line in these joints unless you want to go to jail, and every motherfucker in this state knows it."

While they're talking I keep an eye on Maurice Baltimore. His shirt is open to the solar plexus, the head of Jesus winking in the distance like a gold coin. He sings "Bad to the Bone," then a few funk tunes, ending the set with "It Only Takes a Minute." He minces his feet like James Brown and proclaims that he is Super Bad. He punctuates his patter with lots of Lord Have Mercys.

"Your friend is pretty good," Charlie laughs.

"He's not my friend, Charlie."

"Well, he wants to be." Charlie is still trying to smirk his way out of what happened this morning.

"He's *your* friend," I say. "I think it's you he's after, and he just wanted to get me out of the way."

"You're drunk," Charlie says. "And you're getting on my nerves."

"Did I miss something?" Rodman asks. "Three or four paragraphs? A chapter, maybe?"

"We had a little run-in with that guy, the guy singing," Charlie says. "Nothing really, not a big deal, only Amber doesn't want to let it drop. Amber doesn't know when to let something drop."

"You're the one who started," I say, and turn my back on him.

Meanwhile the band has stopped playing and Rodman calls Maurice Baltimore over. He says, "*Bal*timore."

Maurice comes right up to us. He takes his thin fingers and pinches me on the hip and I go all soft and melty. "Hey, nineteen," says Maurice Baltimore.

"What the hell?" Rodman says.

"It's something I've been meaning to talk to you about," Charlie says. "I thought it could wait."

"Should I fire his ass?" Rodman asks.

"Somebody mind telling me what the charge is?" Maurice asks.

"Tell him, Charlie," Rodman says.

"That just cost you your job," Charlie says. "You didn't know when to quit."

He sidles up close to Charlie, whispers something in his ear then takes a few bills from his pocket and presses them into Charlie's hand. He stands back and looks at me as if no one else is in the room. "You come with me I'll treat you right."

Charlie thinks this is the funniest thing he's ever heard. He opens his hand and lets the money fall.

"You hearing that voice, little queenie?" Maurice says. "I can hear you hearing it."

I take a few steps toward him, like it, take a few steps more.

"This is absurd," Charlie says. He rolls his eyes and punches his hands down into his pockets. "Amber, this is not playtime—"

"He's fired," Rodman says. "Fuhgettaboudit."

"You're fired!" Charlie shrieks. "You come from Baltimore you go back to Baltimore!" He glares at me, sideways, like a dog whose tail has been stepped on.

"Come on," Maurice says to me. His voice is a whisper. "We have to leave now. We have to move on down the line, pret-ty pret-ty la-dy."

And I go. That's the thing. I mean, I don't even think twice about it. Charlie and Rodman are surprised, I guess, but no more than I am.

"He'll follow us," I say, the heels of my Mary Janes snick-snicking like tiny pistol shots on the bare wood floor.

"Of course he will," Maurice says, and holds the door open for me. We go crunching across the gravel parking lot like people with some purpose in life. We get into his car. There are clothes and books and records all heaped in cardboard boxes on the back seat. He lights a cigarette, rolls the window down, looks straight ahead without putting the key in the ignition. Two guys spill out of the place complaining that, for the money they've blown, they could be drunk right now with a hooker on each arm.

"Let's go," I say. "Hurry up!"

"We will, we will," he says, "only wait and see. It only takes a minute, like the song says." We both sit staring at the flood-lit front door of the Florecita Gaming Palace. "Count to sixty," Maurice says and pinches me on the hip again, his fingers moving up my arm, tracing a pattern on my ear, gently undoing the buckle at my throat. "Go ahead and do that for me, pret-ty la-dy," he says, and drops the dog collar into my lap, my thumb brushing the silver-plated spikes while I count *One, two, three, four*—watching the door open and close. I picture Charlie coming through the doors with his goofy smile and his bouncy walk, but by the time I'm finished counting Charlie is still no-where to be seen. A few people trickle in and out and the elec-tric doors open and close. Now that I'm finished counting, I'm not sure what to do.

"That's inside," Maurice Baltimore says, pointing at the Flo-recita Gaming Palace. "Some people like to stay on the inside, while other people prefer to stay on the outside. You and me, I guess we're more like outsiders than insiders."

Maurice flicks his cigarette through the open window. I watch the burning end sail up and land on the empty space of gravel between the car and the front doors. He puts the car in gear and the headlights make crazy shapes on the gravel and then blend in with other headlights as we merge onto the In-terstate. He lights another cigarette and we drive a long time without saying anything, me looking straight ahead and run-ning my fingers over the smooth leather of the dog collar, trac-ing the outline of his fingers on the steering wheel, and while I'm doing that I think about the world, not the one in front of us, the dark one we see and are driving into but the other one, the one behind it, the real one, the one that's on fire and burn-ing day and night.

"All that before, that was inside," he goes on. "Now you out-side. Now you out here with me. How that feel, pretty lady? How that feel to you this very minute of your life?"

Jack Frost

H E CALLS ME BOBBY LIKE HE REALLY KNOWS
me, but I've never laid eyes on this guy before twenty
minutes ago. But anybody can walk up to the blackjack
table where I slap the cards five days a week and look at the
plastic badge on my uniform and call me Bobby, and no intro-
duction is necessary. That's the business I'm in; people want to
recognize and be recognized. It's a business about making people think they're big shots while you fleece them, a con game
more than anything else. And I don't mind it, the familiarity
that is, and going along with it all, the cigar smoke and the stories and really acting like I give a shit if he bets for me or not.
Which I should, because it pays the lion's share of my salary.
But which I don't, because the tips are pooled and divided and
then taxed, a check cut by the casino for you each week, so how
seriously can you take any of it? Most of the time, in fact, I like
to pretend I'm not here, think other thoughts, put my mind in
other places, and I can do it, too, because after all these years I
can deal a game of 21 in my sleep. Which is the only way a person should have to do a job like this, let me tell you.

The customers get on my nerves, to be honest, with their
complaints and their sob stories and their "Come on, Bobby,
let's have a *black*jack this time Bobby, you're not being *nice* to
us Bobby," like I actually have control over any of it. And the
fact is, most people expect to lose—most people, it seems,

want to lose—and yet they'll take it out on you all the same. But once in a while also you'll get a customer who is a little bit considerate, and who might even tell you something fairly interesting, and this guy is one of those. That makes your day go a little easier, and it's only common decency to act like I'm interested, that I'm grateful for the tips, that I enjoy my job and the opportunity to deal to a fine man of the world, a gentleman, a person with style who, although he gets dressed in the dark— the sportcoat that's twenty years out of date, the wide lapels and flower-power tie—is nevertheless a pretty nice person. So I don't mind it. I don't mind thanking him for the money he bets for me—five and sometimes ten dollars placed beside his own quarter bets—and cheering for him to get a blackjack. It's my job, after all, and this guy is better than many. In a toilet like this he's a prince, in fact; but wait, because you're missing the story of how he got his name.

"Oh I was in this country some five years," he's saying. To me, then to the blonde in chair seven. "After the war I did not come here right away, but at first I lived for a time with my mother's relatives in Toronto, Canada. But come here I did, the first chance I got, because I knew I wanted to be American. My English was not bad, having been for ten years in Canada. Still I thought I could improve upon it, and after work three nights of the week I rode a succession of buses from the clothing factory in Brooklyn, where I worked as a cutter, to the basement of a storefront synagogue in Queens. To some of the better students the rabbi would give the moderns that he himself was reading: Joyce and Faulkner, Eliot, Wallace Stevens and Robert Frost. Frost I loved most passionately, for many more reasons than I am able here to go into, but best of all for his famous definition of a poem: 'A momentary stay against confusion.'"

While he's telling this story he's holding up the game, and the woman to his left has lost her money and is standing to leave without hearing the rest of it, and the man to his right is interrupting him and telling him to pay attention to the game. He hits his hand out and breaks, shakes his head, the cigar gripped in his front teeth, a cloud of smoke stinking up the whole table. He promises me we'll try again and says, "You're too young for this Bobby, to remember the Kennedy inauguration, but I was just hitting my stride as an adult and as an American citizen in that election year of 1960, and so when I went to change my name and complete the creation of myself, a new person in a new land, the slate clean, the possibilities fresh, I simply put the names of those two men together and became, on January 29th, 1961, Jack Frost." He looks to either side of him and no one will rise to the bait, or even acknowledge that he just *told* a story, and I smile and fill my face with as much enthusiasm as I can and he gives us the punch line, all suave and ironic and European: "I had no idea, of course, about the nipping at your nose business."

I laugh and he laughs and calls me a dear boy, and the whole thing is very jolly. He adds, almost with regret, "And a name is like a tattoo, in a way; it can't be taken back. I'd paid the money, signed the papers, everything legal."

You run into a player like this once in a while, and they want to be everyone's friend. They overtip and are overly considerate in every way, and so they make up for about a hundred of the backbreaking stiffs who are our average customers, but even so, even though we need them and should be grateful when we see them coming through the door, even at that, you can't help but wonder about them. Why do they think you would care about whatever it is they might want to tell you, and why do they throw so much money at total strangers? So you say the answer is they're paying me to listen, the familiarity, I've said all that. And they're losers, sure, I said that too. But there's more to it, it seems, and I'd like to get at what that more is. The secret side of things.

"My grandson William," he's saying to the black guy in chair one, flashing a plastic-coated picture that dangles from the center of his open wallet. "All American in baseball this year, USC. Out there in California where my daughter and her husband now live." He puts the wallet away as quickly as he's produced it and says to me, "I taught him all the card games, Bobby. Gin rummy, the stud poker games and their variations. The antique games of sweep and fantan." He brings in bits of his life and at times doesn't even seem like he's talking to anybody, but then he'll speak directly to me again, using my name like he's known me for years and years, until he can catch the attention of someone else at the table. The weasely guy who has slipped sideways into the vacant chair to his left; the skinny blonde in chair seven hiding behind the sunglasses. "I myself have loved the card games since I was a boy, in Poland. That was before the war," he says, then turns to me like I'm his slightly stupid grandson. "That's the Second World War, Bobby. You know, way back in history. You know history, Bobby?" he laughs, and pats the green felt tabletop. "*You* know. A girl dates one guy she's a nice girl, two guys she's a girl who likes to have a good time, three guys she's loose, and four she's got history."

Everybody at the table laughs, especially Jack Frost, although the joke is not really all that funny. I'm being paid to laugh, so I laugh.

"Charming," Jack Frost says, puffing the cigar and riffling the short stack of red and green chips that used to be five hundred dollars. "Absolutely charming. Such a great game: a great game and a great country. But I was saying. I learned these games, back in Poland when I was a boy, before the war, Bobby. Have I told you this, how I learned, or rather how I taught myself?"

"No, sir. I don't think I've heard that one." I've never seen this guy in my life, so how could he have told me anything? Still, maybe he has me confused with somebody else. After a while all these players start to look alike, so why shouldn't the reverse also be true? You can look down a row of games in here and see all the dealers lined up like stuffed animals in an arcade, our uniforms and even our expressions most of the time exactly the same.

"In our town, Bobby," he says, "I lived with my family in a large apartment that looked out on a row of brightly painted storefronts that ran from the train station to the town square, with its statue of some long-dead Polish nobleman whose name unfortunately escapes me at this moment. In those days, as in the America of that time, from what I've read, the men of the town socialized in the barber shop, and they had a back room where there was always a card game in progress. I'd stand at the door, pretending to do something else, and I'd watch them, and listen, by the hour. Just like that I learned all the games." He places the burning cigar in the ashtray, accepts a scotch and water from the hovering waitress. "I told you two small cubes, and no damned lemon peel!" he scolds the waitress, then tips her five dollars for a five-dollar drink.

"Oh, those were good days, Bobby," he tells me, and seems

almost about to grab my hand as it lays first an ace of clubs then a queen of diamonds down in front of him. "My youth, Bobby, such as it was." Then adds, "Ah, bleckjeck, sure, when I have the small money up."

He plays three more hands without saying anything and, even though his luck hasn't been great, he bets a few red chips for me, then a few more. I drop the nickels into the plastic box that's bolted to the backside of the table. Jack Frost's money rattles around in the empty space where the tips from the other customers should be but are not.

"You were in Poland before the war?" the black guy in chair one barks out. "That's something. That's really *some*thing. And here you are today. Right here on this spot!"

"Sure, sure," Jack Frost says. "I always think of those days, the card games the men in the town would have. They made pinochle games with matchsticks, and sometimes they got out chips for a real poker game. The boys would crowd around the doorway in the evening and we would make our own bets, which of the men would be the big winner, who would be scolded by his wife for losing too much. Then later, in the camp, I even organized a few card games. Not to bet, of course—we had nothing—but only to pass the time. I'd take bits of rag, splinters of wood, anything I could get my hands on, and make a deck of cards. Perhaps that's why I love a game of cards to this very day. In the camp the saddest time of day was late afternoon, when people in the world begin to think about family, dinner, the comforts of home—and we of course had none of those things. I'd sit with my brother Theo in the darkening barracks, and with one eye I'd deal out the game, and with the other I'd watch for the guards."

"Incredible!" the black guy whose name turns out to be Lonnie says. He is a tourist, by the looks of him, a hat and Bermuda shorts man. A bet for fun man, not caring. "That's like something out of history!"

"Sure it is," Jack says, delighted that someone is listening. "I'm a very historical individual. But history is all around us, my friend." He waves his hand in the air and looks around, and I stop for a moment to look with him. Lonnie looks also, like he's being taken on a guided tour. The theme of our casino is the French Revolution, and just as Jack is waving his hand in the air a cocktail waitress in a powdered wig and hoopskirt floats by and asks him if he'd like another drink, and he tells her no, it's late in the afternoon and he should go upstairs to his room and rest for an hour before dinner. When she disappears back in the crowd he says, "You understand history, Bobby? A mingling together is history. The important and the unimportant indiscriminately heaped." He waves a thin arm in the smoky air. "In the midst of all this activity an apparition from the past descends as if from above to offer me two fingers of scotch whiskey in a false-bottom glass. You see now how history operates?" he asks, examining the short end of his cigar and the remainder of his drink, the thin line of scotch shifting and tilting at the bottom of the glass. "Marie Antoinette brings me a drink of Scotch whiskey and Robespierre deals out a game of cards and then later I go upstairs and Louis the Sun King brings me filet mignon steak and a tossed salad. Because the truth is that I am in the past as much as they are: I just got an extension."

He replaces the cigar in the ashtray and stubs it out. He arches forward suddenly on his toes to peer over the back edge of the table into the tip box, then plops back into the ivory-colored chair. "Not bad, Bobby," he says, and I look and I guess it's about a hundred dollars I've made from him in less than an hour, while no one else at the table has given me so much as a hello and goodbye. But I'm used to it, and I don't look at things that way. I try not to take anything that goes on in here personal. A lot of the time, in fact, it seems that there's this robot who comes in here and does this job so that the real person, Bobby, can look after more important things, plan his life, think about girls, decide on whether to apply to night college or not. I went into the casino right out of high school, and I guess I've been here longer than I thought I would. I still live at home, and my mother is always on me about losing weight, starting college, *do*ing something. She'll pull out my old toys once in a while, just to really put it in my eye. The plastic doctor's set, and the compound microscope in its wooden box, the glass slides of animal blood and insect parts still wrapped in tissue paper. She'll take this stuff out and spread it on the dining room table and ask in this heartbroken voice why I'm no longer interested in such things. That's, like, so completely unfair of her, and more than once I've stormed out of the house and down to the Happy Clam, the dive bar at the corner of our street, to give her an idea about what I may or may not be currently interested in. But she means it for my own good, I guess you could say. A mother will stop at nothing, as far as that's concerned. I can't seem to make her understand that a job is just a job, a way to exchange time for money, and it doesn't really matter very much what you do. You're not supposed to like it: that's why they call it work.

"Thank you sir," I say. "Thanks for coming to see me today, Mr. F."

"An appointment with you is like an appointment with the

undertaker, Bobby," he says, deadpan. A few people at the table
snicker and Lonnie laughs and looks at the few red chips he has
left in front of him and says, "That's the truth, too."

"No," Jack tells him, "just a joke. A little private joke. We're
old friends, Bobby and me. In life we're all strangers on a train,
as the expression goes, but in death one finds that everybody
knows everybody. Therefore good luck to you, sir, and to everybody!" He raises the tiny puddle of scotch in the air and an-
nounces, "To the nightmare of history, then. From which we all,
sooner or later, willing or unwilling, must awake!" He pours the
few drops of whiskey into his open mouth. He peels the soggy
green Macanudo seal from the cold cigar without tearing it and
places it into the top pocket of his shirt.

And then he takes the small pile of chips he has left, a few
hundred dollars, and he pushes the whole thing into the circle
in front of him. He wins, stacks it up, wins again, almost twice
as much as what he started out with. For a while, at least, he
becomes reckless; he stacks and stacks. "Table max!" I call out
to the floorman, who marches up in his black suit to see what
all the fuss is about. All the nickel players at the table *ooh* and
ahh, like he's made high rollers of them. Like they're all in on
it. In ten or fifteen minutes the pendulum swings back again,
though, just like it always does, and he loses everything. He
nods happily, stands up, leans toward Lonnie, all the way across
the table so that the right sleeve of his jacket pulls back like a
bathrobe might, and in the center of his hairless forearm is a
blurry line of numbers. Then they're shaking hands all around.
Lonnie and Jack, the weasely guy who was trying to ignore him
the whole time until now, the skinny blonde who is in here as
much as I am but still won't hit a sixteen against a face card.

Jack Frost wishes us all the best life has to offer, even as he trails
away in the direction of the elevators. I follow him for a second
with my eyes before I lose him in the crowd. I clap my hands
to show the cameras I'm not stealing anything, adjust my uniform, take a deep breath and get ready to deal the next hand.

"That's something," the tourist guy named Lonnie says.
"That's really something."

"It is," I say. "He's a nice guy. He's like a character out of
history."

"Yeah, man. And A-men to that. The history of the *world*, if
you understand where I'm coming from." He tips his hat then,
a red cotton baseball cap with a large black *X* embroidered in
the peak.

The customers who had been sitting around Jack Frost drop
out, one at a time, and then finally it's me and Lonnie, and at last
I take his few nickels and the game goes dead.

"That's right," Lonnie laughs, swaggering back out into the
crowd. "Now I'm history, too!"

These jokers come in and forget about everything for a couple of hours, but then the money is gone and the time is up and
they have to go back out into it. So let them go. As for me, I can
use the break. I spread the cards while I consider what I'm going to eat on my next break, what I'm going to do on my days
off. Things you think, just getting through the day. I check my
watch, look around the room. I look out into the aisle and see,
kind of, what Jack Frost meant about history. How it all swarms
together. All the layers, down and down. There are waitresses
in hoop skirts and powdered wigs, floating like moths below
the lights that beat down on the green felt where the hands
move day and night and the money is won or lost. There are

men clogging the aisles in leisure suits, jogging suits, business
suits. Women in evening wear, sportswear, wash and wear.
There is the noise of the crowd like the surf rushing and breaking, and mixed in with it the sound of cold cash as it circulates
endlessly through the machines, across the tables, down the
drain. I look up into the bank of mirrors across the aisle and in
the smoke-clouded glass I can see all the dealers in a line, laying out hands, taking bets, counting money. At the end of that
line is me. Not me, exactly, but the eighteenth-century foot-
man I send out into the world each day to earn my living: white
puffed shirt, blue tri-corner hat, red sash cut tight across the
girth of him. He nods his head, blinks his dusty eyes. I wave my
hand; wriggle my fingers.

Upstairs Room

I'D BEEN GONE THREE DAYS, SHACKED IN WEST Atlantic City with a bad-tempered cocktail waitress named Irene Smith, but Irene Smith was not entirely the point of it, as Irene herself eventually learned. I called and said I was coming back to pick up my things.

"I'll fall on bended knee when you arrive," she said to me over the phone.

I came up the stairs and stood for a moment inside the door of her sitting room. It's a spare room we fixed with a TV and a beat-up love seat, plus a pair of old highboys I had pulled the drawers out of and set up as bookcases for her romance novels, which she reads by the bushel basketfuls. I had found them, the highboys, on my way to the job one Monday morning. Somebody had thrown them out in the rain, the two of them, where they would get picked up by the trash men. I loaded them into the back of the pickup and threw a tarp over them, worked my shift, dried them off with rags in the garage after supper. When I looked up she was standing inside the door with that plastic rain hat of hers tied loose around her hair. She had cleaned up and done the dishes and then come out after me with two bottles of Pabst and a bowl filled up with potato chips. It was green Depression glass, the bowl, and I had found it at a sidewalk sale on my way to do a job on a yard for some guy named MacCaulley.

I should explain that on weekends I do landscaping work
to supplement my regular job of auto mechanic for a fat guy
named Sims. Well, I was doing this guy MacCaulley's yard, and
the mower broke down on me. I hit a pine cone and there was
a screeching noise, followed by a sheet of blue smoke, and then
she died on me, right then and there. I use junk mowers picked
up out of the Shopper's Guide and out of the trash, too. They almost all of them have those two-stroke Briggs and Stratton en-
gines in them, and they're easy to work on. I get a few months'
work out of the thing and it's practically free, if you don't count
my time working on it, which I don't. It's my time and I can
spend it however I want, and besides that I like it, taking something somebody else thinks is useless and getting some use out
of it. So I had to break her down right there on the spot and she
was spent, the whole thing, melted down. I had another mower
on the truck of course, and after a while MacCaulley came out.
He said, "How about fixing that thing on your own time? You
got another mower on the truck." So I told him, "Come to that,
how about getting yourself a man who charges you twenty-five
a week and then beats you for fertilizer and lime he never uses
on top of that?" MacCaulley went back in the house and shut
the door behind him.

This was right after I came back from there. The bowl cost
twenty-five cents, and I'd brought it in while she was out of the
house over at her mother's place. I put it on that little gate-leg
table the previous owners of the house had left in back of the
garage. I filled the bowl with tap water, then went out back and
picked two daisies. I remember I stood over the small bed by
the back steps trying to decide if I should pick one or two of
them, trying to think of how big the bowl was, how many petals I'd need and all like that. Finally I picked two, just to be on

the safe side. I sprinkled the petals on the surface of the water
inside the green glass bowl. I wanted to get it exactly right, and
when I finished it looked like one of those Japanese paintings,
you know, the odd patterns running here and there. I stood
there picturing how her eyes would light up when she saw it.
When I looked down I had two daisy stems in my hands, and
one of the stems had three petals left. I pressed them in a book,
a middle volume of an encyclopedia which I have somewhere.
And this bowl, which she was crazy about because of the way I
had given it to her, was the same one she brought into the garage that night.

She came out to where I was drying off those highboys with
a bunch of rags, after she had done the dishes and dried them
and put everything back in its place the way I like it done. She
came inside the garage, I remember, and it was still raining and
the garage door was rolled all the way up but there was no wind,
and the rain was coming straight down in sheets and snicker-
ing off the small slab of concrete between the garage and the
house. She had that green bowl filled with chips in one hand
and two bottles of Pabst and an opener in the other and a little
umbrella tilted forward over the chips and caught under the
arm of her raincoat. I took the umbrella and closed it and took
the beer and chips out of her hands and she stood there for a
minute while she untied the rain hat and fluffed her hair and
tried to find a shiny surface to look into before I might really
see her. It had rained that entire day, and she had on that plastic rain hat because she'd been to the beauty parlor and didn't
want to spoil her hairdo. I stopped what I was doing and we
stood there, drinking the cold beers and eating the chips out of
the green glass bowl.

"What're you going to do with them?" she asked me, and

she went over to where they stood against the wall and ran her hand down along the back and sides. You could see she was really interested, and not inquiring just to be polite. You could see she thought I was pretty wonderful, too, to take something like that out of the rain and do something with it nobody else would think to do, even she couldn't guess what. We stood there, smiling at each other and drinking the beer. "I'm going to pull the drawers out of those," I told her. "Permanently, I mean, and strip them and stain them maple and put that real hard clearcoat on them. If you look inside you can see the way they made the furniture back then. The drawers don't sit on cheap plywood runners and plastic rollers; the whole compartment for every drawer is completely enclosed, and it's solid wood. Not the same kind of wood as the outside, of course, but pretty good. I'll refinish them and put your novels in them, and you can have a little sitting area with your books, and a sofa, maybe, that brass pole lamp I got from MacCaulley last spring, and a TV set. You can have a place of your own like I have this place. We can cozy up in there some nights when we don't feel like being downstairs in the living room, and we can watch a little TV. It won't be a color TV but it'll be fun and different, and even a little bit like we're away on a vacation somewhere, the two of us in this quaint spot with this funny black-and-white TV." She got kind of smoochy on me, just then. I stuffed the rags into the highboys every which way I could, and we called it a night.

And so I was thinking all this when I came in on her sitting there in that back room like some hothouse flower, watching a black-and-white TV set when she could've been downstairs, watching color. Next to her the little spotted dog I'd found and given to her was sitting up, blinking. I had given it to her on account of her age, because she couldn't have any children and she was feeling like she needed something little to be tender toward. The dog was blinking with the flickering shapes the TV made in the dark room. She was sitting there, staring at the TV and swishing the ice around in her drink and then chewing the cubes, making that shivering noise with her teeth that drives me up a wall, and which I've told her not to do in front of me. The little pie-dog turned his head when he saw my shadow come into the room before I did, and then when he saw it was me he went back to watching the TV. Those black-and-white TVs throw heavy shadows in a room and it's creepy-like, sometimes, to come in on her like that, just her and the little dog sitting side by side like a couple of dolls, and the volume on that old Motorola turned down low, on account of she gets those migraines, and those long shadows washing over them like some picture pulled down out of the spirit world, all blue and dark and wavy.

"You ought to get some use out of the good set," I said as I came inside the quiet room. "It's a nine-hundred-dollars Sony."

I set my coat on the floor and opened the top button of my shirt. I sat down on the sofa next to her with the dog between us and a minute passed before she said anything.

"I like it up here," she said finally, as if she'd just noticed me that second sitting next to her. "It's cozy. You fixed this room for me." She smiled at me then, and took a long swallow of the highball she had on the table by her left hand.

"I fixed this room for you," I said, nice and even, "but I didn't intend for you to sit in it drinking highballs day and night."

"I didn't know you had a booklet with rules in it made up

when you fixed this room for me," she said, still smiling. "If that's how it is, then I'd at least like to get a copy."

I glared at her shadow and she glared back at mine. Right there I wanted to stand back up and wipe that smile off her drunken face. I raised my open hand up next to my ear, expecting even more lip, but she only said, "I've gone through this twice before. I can't go through it again. Joe—" And her voice trailed off, not knowing what else to say. I could see that she was breathing hard and her chest and arms were heaving under the thin housecoat, and after a minute one hand, the hand without the drink in it, went up to smooth and primp the rollers in her hair. It made me want to protect her and take care of her; it made me want to think of better times.

To this day I think about this one time, after we first met. It was a hot day, we packed my truck and drove to the beach with a picnic lunch and two six packs. I remember we had the lunch and one of the sixes and she wanted to swim. I'm not much on that and I burn if I'm not covered. But she wanted to go in and I remember how I sat on that lawn chair with a cold beer and a cigarette, watching her swim. She splashed around in those breakers like some bathing beauty in an old newsreel, a bathing cap and a candy-striped bathing suit. I sat watching as she pranced the waves, and I remember like it was something I pressed in a book and saved how she looked and how damn happy I was about everything, another chance come along so late in life after all the opportunities missed and the mistakes made, a marriage of twenty-two years in pieces behind me, two kids of mine who barely speak to me over some of the things that went on, and her smiling at me and waving, and how I told myself, *Now remember this, you. Hang onto this, you.* I had

a line in, just for the sake of it, and I didn't even realize I had
something on the other end of it until I heard the drag on that
old Penn Squidder start clicking off, so that by the time I stood
up and took the pole in my hands that fish had already stripped
off fifty yards of line and was moving deep and steady sideways
beneath the breaking waves. I burned hell out of my thumb
slowing it down before I could get the drag tightened and set
the hook, the split bamboo pole bent almost double, and finally
I got the fish beached—a late summer striper, just legal—and
it laid half-drowned at the place where the seafoam scudded
at the high-water mark. A stiff wind had kicked up out of the
northeast, breathing the waves all the way downbeach so that
you could feel that first whisper of fall in the air, the dying and
the regret, and she said to me before I even knew she was there
but at the same time like she had been there the entire time I
was fighting and then beaching that fish, "Oh, Joe, it's so beautiful. You're not going to keep it, are you?"

   I still like to think about that fish, the rippling black stripes
and the silver-white belly and the way the spiny back chafed
for a second against my foot while the dorsal expanded and he
righted himself in the fast moving water. The way it felt the
exact second he was off the sand and swimming again—the
weightlessness that was not the fish's absence, exactly, but the
fish feeling my absence—feeling free. Or something like that. I
don't know what I'm trying to say. We changed inside the truck
and drove with the windows rolled down through the late afternoon. We had boiled crabs at some newspaper-on-the-table
type of place, and I guess there was sex later and everything
like that but it was those few things, the way that fish felt on
the top of my foot and the way the surf strained and pushed all

the way downbeach and the way her voice sounded in my ear, I remember all that, the happiest day of my life.

I sold my trailer in McKee City and we got some money together and put it down on a house she'd found up at the north end of Limit, an old brick-colored Cape Cod at the narrow flooding tip of the island, which is how we got it cheaper. We arranged a small wedding with a few friends from my job, her mother and sister, no costumes. We wore our own clothes and had it in the nondenominational chapel they have on the boardwalk, the one next door to the Taj Majal. I still have the suit I bought for it, and I wear it on occasion. It's midnight-blue sharkskin with a white shirt and burgundy tie. We went to the men's store in the casino for it, and it cost over three hundred dollars, and I'll always remember the look on her face when I tried it on, that I was doing that for her. "Joe," she said, and didn't say anything else for a minute. "You're handsome, Joe. I'm marrying a handsome guy."

Of course the salesman agreed. We went and got her a dress after that, then had lunch at Caesar's, a Japanese steak restaurant, someplace she'd read about in the paper and wanted to try. You've never seen anybody as happy as she was that day: happier, even, I think, than on the wedding day. We had a bottle of wine and she ordered the most expensive thing off the menu, and it cost a bundle. She beamed the entire time, but I remember thinking, *This is our celebration. Then we go back to our regular lives. I hope you understand that.* I never did say that, not to spoil things, but she never did understand that, either. She thought it would go on that way, like that day at the beach and then later when she came in on me that night in the garage with the beers and there was this *feeling*, all of a sudden.

Those are the things that make up a life, I wanted to tell her, but they're not all of life. You don't get that every day.

Because I think she thought you did. She thought a lunch like that with a thirty dollar bottle of wine was something people did every week, or just whenever they felt like it. I was only a little kid in Depression times, but it stayed with me. I remember my father, strapped all the time and sick with worry and regret right up until the night he went down to the corner variety for a cigar, and we never saw him again. It stays with you, that kind of stuff. You're always waiting for the bottom to fall out. You save a dollar where you can, and extravagance sickens you a little. You think of the waste. You would never take a cab where you could walk it or hop a bus. You'd never buy new if you could buy used, and this isn't about money or being cheap; it's about living real and saving for a rainy day. It's about a certain way you are, a way you see things, and you can't help it.

In the quiet room I could hear the steady grinding and blowing of the oil furnace and the steam pipes as they popped and pinged inside the plaster walls. The first cold night in October and she had the furnace turned full up. I could feel the heat rising upstairs inside the room and all around us. "*Joe,*" she said, and began to fuss with the rollers in her hair. The dog stirred and whimpered. I stood up then, before she would have a chance to say anything else, and as I went for my coat the sudden movement upset the reception from the rabbit ears that I used so that I didn't have to pay for another cable outlet, and the vertical hold on that old set gave out and began to roll the picture sideways.

"You, Joe!" she screamed.

She stood up in her place and without moving her feet she

reached up and slapped me once, hard as she could manage, across the side of my face. I almost laughed at the soft weight of her hand and the little dull sting of it. "Why do you have to throw it all away?" she said to me, the television rolling black bars across her face and the little pie-dog on the sofa barking like there was no tomorrow as I stabbed an arm into my winter coat.

I thought about this other time when I was out cutting the grass in our yard this past spring after we'd moved into the house and gone through a cold winter there together. I had one of my typical junk mowers, and I was out there running it over the crab grass the last owner had left me, and it up and died. She saw me standing there with my toolbox and came outside and stood beside me while I cursed over the thing half an hour in the chilly afternoon. Finally she said, "Get in the truck, let's go." I don't know why but I didn't ask any questions. I went into the house and got the keys, my light windbreaker, locked the house up and came back outside. She was already in the cab of the truck with her purse on her lap, looking straight ahead. She didn't smile or talk the entire time except to give me directions, and I didn't say anything, I trusted her that wherever we were going was where we should be going.

When she pointed left at the mall parking lot I said, "Sears?"

"Sure," she told me, and was already down out of the truck and walking across the parking lot while I locked the truck and caught up with her. "It's where America shops."

She took me by the hand down the waxed linoleum aisle, past the washing machines and the refrigerators and the microwaves and the color TVs until we came to Lawn and Garden, and when we stopped there I said, "No. We don't need this. I can get by all right without this. I appreciate the idea."

"I have money of my own," she told me. "I have a bank account. I worked many years at Spencer Gifts placing whoopee cushions into cardboard boxes. So I don't want to hear about what we need and don't need. I'm half of this. This is what I want to do with my half."

The salesman came up and he went through the usual song and dance, but she was tight-fisted, not like she had been that day in the store over my suit, letting them know we would spend whatever they told us to. She asked questions, price and warranty, and I stood there with my mouth shut, letting her do everything. When she was satisfied that it was a square deal she paid by check, and the salesman with his pencil holder and his clip-on tie gave me a hand with it out to the truck. I went over it in my mind why I was driving home with a lawn mower I could buy used out of the paper for an eighth of what she'd just paid, but when we got it home and I took it down off the back of the truck then I knew why. The day had turned damp and foggy but I ran that thing up and down the stupid patch of scrub grass that was my yard, happy as a kid on Christmas morning. A pale, silvery sun was sliding into the public docks at the end of our street by the time I'd emptied the last bag of grass. I remember standing inside the garage, cleaning the new mower up—there was a fine film of dirt on the red engine cover, and wet grass already stuck up under the stainless housing—but it was getting dark, and I could hear her thin voice calling to me through the open doorway. I waited then, held my breath and didn't answer while I watched her shadow rise and then tilt sideways on the slab of darkening concrete. After a few minutes she went back inside the house, and I pulled the garage door closed and walked down the block with my hands in my pockets.

At the end of our street, set away from the public docks in a tangle of reeds, is a dive bar called the Happy Clam. That's where I found a woman whose name turned out to be Irene Smith, sitting at the bar all by herself, high up on a stool—you've seen women like that, attractive but a little past it, and you can see that sometimes when they smile, desperate-like but brassing it out, their eyes a little wild and their nostrils flared and their teeth when they smile like a horse's teeth, like they're trying to outrun whatever life has in store for them, and they know they can't but that doesn't stop them from running all the same, and it doesn't stop them from enjoying it, either.

Have You Seen This Girl?

DARCY COMES ON A BUS, ACROSS AMERICA she travels, smiling face and daisy-colored hair and chin cleft like a broken heart.

"Hi Darcy," Howard says. "Hi Darcy Darce Darce Darce Darce!"

"Hi Howard," Darcy says. "Hi there Howie How How How How!"

"We don't have much space in this place," I hear myself saying. "Darcy will have to sleep on the couch." I didn't want her to come at all but Howard said, "It's my sister, Christine. What do you want me to do?"

Darcy put in some bad time with a guy in Absecon, New Jersey. Darcy is always putting in bad time with some guy in a place like Absecon, New Jersey. She's always calling Howard up and Howard is always telling me about it, poor Darcy, the tough time she's always having. My best friend Martha met her one time at our apartment here in Las Vegas, a year ago, and told me that Darcy looked like bad news.

"There are bad news people in the world," Martha said, "and Darcy is surely one of them." Martha sometimes acts like a fortune teller, and once in a while she does hit on things. But it isn't dread so much as that I haven't been feeling so hot these days; it's become increasingly apparent to me that there is a noticeable gap between the girl who goes around with my name and the girl who sits up there in the control booth, all by herself, behind the instrument panel. Things have not been so great between me and Howard since we moved to Las Vegas, over a year ago I guess it's been, and it's a bit much when you realize you're supporting a guy who no longer even touches you, and that drugs have pretty much taken over every consideration and decision, and that you don't want to stop snorting meth because it's the only thing that makes you feel *halfway* human, and all this is not bad enough but now you've got to put up with your boyfriend's flaky sister, too.

In this way, in the middle of this journey I call my life, Darcy arrives with a few things stuffed in a cloth suitcase and a mouse under her left eye. "I'm tired of men," Darcy says. "I've given up on them completely. They bring out my bad side. At the end he couldn't even get it up: he was using a strap-on."

"How demeaning," Howard says.

"For whom?" Darcy says. "Demeaning for whom? And if I'm gonna swing like that then what do I need guys for in the first place?"

"I think that's for you to decide," I say.

"I'm gonna raise my living standards and move uptown," Darcy says. She's always saying things like that. What can you say to something like that?

She says: "In the end I objectified him with a gaze of indifference."

"Oh, well," I say. "Is that when he busted you in the face?"

"Christine!" Howard says. He clucks his tongue. "*So* insensitive."

"I thought we were discussing this intelligently," I say.

"We were we were," Darcy says. "I'm gonna get a girl a soft girl so my life can be soft from now on. My life's too hard," she says, smoking the last of our pot then picking the crumbs from a box of Frosted Mini-Wheats.

I serve cocktails in a dump two blocks off Freemont called the Emerald City. I walk the quarter slots area in a tits-and-ass Dorothy costume, emerald thong and ruby-encrusted pumps. On my way back to the service bar I stop outside the poker parlor to watch Martha. Her blue eyes flash from behind the dark screen of her hair as she deals the cards; she pitches them, saying, "Queen to the ace, Jack to the trey. Ace bets."

Martha came here from Argentina when she was a little girl, so she barely has an accent. She spent her childhood someplace else, I don't remember where. In Las Vegas nobody you meet is actually ever from Las Vegas. I started out my life in New Orleans, born to a musical family, though I inherited none of their talent, my Mama still there, moved out with friends to a houseboat on Lake Pontchartrain, my Daddy traveled on to parts unknown. Howard and I moved here from Jupiter Beach, Florida, and before that we were undergraduates at NYU, where Howard got his bachelor's in film and I lost interest in getting mine. I no longer cared about film as story, the image as a fundamentally accurate representation of reality; I lost faith in the very idea of narrative coherence.

Meanwhile, Howard is working on his MFA at UNLV. They gave him the full boat plus a stipend, which means I pay all the bills and Howard can kid himself that he's holding up his end while he sits around in a ratty bathrobe all day, snorting meth and reading Derrida. We've taken up residence in a sprawling, sixties-modern apartment complex called Western Winds while Howard works on his second project, which I'm hoping will finally give us some sort of a payday. The first film starred

Darcy and is called *Have You Seen This Girl?*, the story of a wild
and sexy chick in the Big Apple and how she turns into a "de-
monette"—cloven feet and vestigial tail—and becomes even
more popular as a result. The point being that "evil" is sexy, attractive, the stuff of real life, while "good" is a bit like Robert
Stack—a recurring device in the movie, an actor dressed up to
look like Robert Stack speaking from an open casket: *Have you
seen this girl? She was last seen, etc.*—dependable, essentially
decent, but embalmed. The film won fourth place two years
ago at Sundance and was distributed for, like, two weeks in
Seattle.

For his second film Howard was going to make a movie
called *Casino*, until he remembered there already is a movie
called *Casino*. He changed the name to *Blackjack*. It's a movie
about the gaming industry here in Las Vegas, how people want
to get numb and stay numb: how the blackjack of American
culture knocks you permanently unconscious. When he went
to start shooting, though, he found out that none of the casinos
would allow so much as a box camera on the casino floor. He
rigged a camera in my handbag. He conducted interviews with
casino people punching out at the time clock, talking about
the drudgery that passes for entertainment, the desperation of
the customers, how so many of the dealers, who should know
better, have gambling habits. Martha's boyfriend Justin is the
star this time. He's dealt blackjack at the Mirage for five years
and can tell you stories, although after a while they all blend together. Most of the footage is of Justin in his dealer's costume,
going through his day, giving interviews, taking drugs, reciting Shelley and Keats. Then he becomes an obnoxious gambler
in a plaid sportcoat who also happens to give interviews, take

drugs, and recite Shelley and Keats. Howard says it's all about the transformation of experience, imaginative flight, things that turn unexpectedly into their opposites.

When our shift is over Martha and I meet up with Howard and Darcy for Tex-Mex. Darcy asks Martha all these questions about being a poker dealer and working downtown.

"I want a job like that," she tells Martha. "You can get lost in it."

"Except that you don't always want to be lost," Martha tells her. "You might think you do—"

"I do," she says. She twists the frayed ends of her hair and drinks Margaritas one after the other. "Is it not all right for me to get lost?" she asks. "Do I owe somebody and a bill is in the mail? How come it's never a check that's in the mail? I'm tired of living in the negative numbers."

She smokes my cigarettes, one after the other. I say, "Don't you ever breathe oxygen?"

She says: "This conversation is like oxygen, Christine."

She follows Martha off to the women's room.

Howard says, "Maybe Darcy is suited to this place. Maybe the big thing is that she got out of New Jersey."

When they come back they are bumping up against each other and giggling like teenagers at a pajama party. They point at one another, laughing, and say, "You! You!"

"Darcy's all right," Martha says the next day to me in the Emerald City cafeteria. "I had her all wrong."

"You think so?" I say, stubbing out my cigarette. The air conditioner is up in the cafeteria and I'm freezing cold in the Dorothy outfit. "I don't think so," I say. "I think she's big trouble. I think she sucks up all the energy around her. I don't think they manufacture enough oxygen for little Darcy."

"She's been through a lot," Martha says. "I talked to her about it. We're going for Chinese tonight."

"Really?"

"When she looks at me," Martha says, looking at me, "I think she really cares about what I have to say. That's so rare. She's really somebody I can talk to."

"Is that right?" I say.

"That's right," Martha says. "And you could be a little nicer to her, Christine."

"Sure," I say. "I get to be nice and you get to eat dim sum."

Monday night we finish our shift and meet up for Tex-Mex. We all have Tuesdays and Wednesdays off so that we can hang out together and snort crystal meth, and we always prepare for our binge with Mexican food and margaritas. Martha's boyfriend Justin is there with Martha and it's me and Howard except that Darcy is the fifth wheel. She asks Justin lots of questions and then when he answers she puts him down. "That's absurd," she says. "You know nothing!" she shrieks, then punches his arm, one-two. Justin doesn't know what to do with this. When Darcy goes to the women's room Martha tags along after her.

"Hey, wait up," Martha says, all breathy and pert.

Justin says, "Howard, is your sister an insane person?"

"Naw, just kind of different. She's like an actress who does Darcy more than she really is Darcy."

"Yeah?"

"Darcy is like film," Howard says. "In film you take what's on this side and put it on the other side. Everybody can experience it but nobody can touch it."

"Well," he says, "she's getting on my nerves. And I don't think she wants me around anyway. I thought she did, but now I don't think she does."

"Justin is bitter," Howard says to me. "Darcy gave him the come on and then the brush off before he even had time to change his shorts. She's a quick one, little Darcy is," he explains to Justin. "No moss. Strictly Teflon: a non-stick surface. Text without context."

She's flipped on him from the first night when he met her in our apartment. That first night Justin was all over Darcy. She was wearing her usual thrift store trash, black velvet gloves up to the elbow. He gave her the round-eyed sympathy routine. He gave her the I'll Be the Mirror That You Can Gaze at Your Lovely Self In routine. They were in the kitchen together at one point and we could overhear noises. The light went out and Darcy's voice said: "Please don't, please. Don't please. You're hurting me." Justin ducked his head around the corner and held out his hands. Darcy continued: "Please don't. Please. I'm scared. You're hurting me." Everybody thought that was so funny.

"It's now time for me to take speed and tell you the story of my life," Darcy said, coming out of the kitchen with a water glass of Chardonnay, even though we have stemware. Darcy shook her little pudding ass while everybody snorted the lines so pure they almost jumped off the mirror into our noses.

"I'm all ears," Justin said.

"Me too," Martha said.

"I don't mind reruns once in a while," Howard said.

"Oh Howard," Darcy said, and threw her velvet-rope arms around his neck. "Oh Howie How How How How."

There was the guy she lost her virginity to at age fourteen but before that there were the eleven guys she almost lost her virginity to at ages ten through thirteen and a half.

When Martha and Darcy come back from the women's room they are wiping their noses with the backs of their hands and talking about all the men in Darcy's life, as if that same conversation has continued from last week to this. The next time they go to the women's room together they disappear and we don't see them for two days. Justin stays with us and we snort meth off my framed Ingmar Bergman poster (an original *Seventh Seal* poster intended for theater distribution) and talk about Darcy. Since she hit town it seems there is no oxygen for anybody but Darcy. Even when she's not in the room, people talk about her. Now even Justin says, "Your sister is a flake, but she sure has something. I wonder where they went off to. I'd just love to know where they went off to."

One by one the lines leap off the picture glass and vanish without a trace. We tilt our noses skyward, we clench our jaws, we get the little tinglies in our scalps like people on the verge of an illumination. Everything in the room seems to rise up, brighter and brighter. Howard says, "This is now. Now now now now now."

Coincident with the arrival of Darcy I begin to have bad dreams. There is a furry little creature that follows me around in these dreams. The creature acts like my pet, and I act friendly toward it, but I'm secretly afraid of it. It's most important, though, that the creature never find out I'm scared of it. If it ever finds out, terrible things will happen, although I'm not sure, in terms of the dreamlogic, what they might be. The sleep at the end of being wired on speed for a couple of days is cold and black, like falling into a well. On the fringe of this dark circular space the monster roams, furry and hostile.

It's important we stay on good terms, even though I hate and fear it. What can all this mean?

"She's got a vibrator the size of a sixteen ounce beer can," Martha says to me on break that Friday. "You have just no idea."

"I didn't know you were interested in that kind of thing."

"Neither did I. Oh, neither did *I*," Martha says, and widens her baby-blues. "But she's so sweet. Do you think I should tell Justin?"

"Tell Justin what, exactly?" is what I'd like to know.

"That I'm leaving him for Darcy, of course."

"Take it easy, Christine," Howard says. "Let her go and live with Martha if that's what she wants to do. And I thought you wanted her out of here. I thought you wanted things back the way they were." He comes close, puts a hand to my cheek and the other in the small of my back. "God, honey, it's gonna be sweet when we can make noise in the night the way that we used to and get the colored lights going," he says in his best Stanley Kowalski. People who make literary allusions get on my nerves, and Howard is beginning to get on my last Christine nerve. Meanwhile, Martha was my friend. Now it's all Darcy, morning noon and night Darcy. Martha thinks I should be happy for her. She says she finally found what she was after in this life.

"Maybe she has," Howard says. "Who are you to say?"

Howard turns the music up loud and starts jumping around the room.

"She's got low self-esteem," I say. "A shame-based condition."

"Huh? What was that?"

"Nothing, Howard. Don't worry about it."

"How do you think Justin feels?" I ask Martha the next day. "I mean, how do you think the guy feels?"

"Oh, he doesn't care about me," Martha says. "It's about sex for him. I'm, like, just another pretty face. Plus, don't forget, Christine, he went after her first."

"Darcy is a sexual predator," I say, beginning to lose patience. "She uses and discards people because of her own feelings of inadequacy. She feels so bad, she has to make everybody else around her feel bad too. Can't you see that, Martha?"

"Oh no," Martha says in this breathy little voice. "Not in the least. Darcy is this wonderfully creative girl who gives so much of herself in every moment that all you want to do when you're with her is make her happy. That's the only thing in the world that matters." Her face gets a twisty look that seems intended to convey an image of happiness in bloom but which only succeeds in making her look feebleminded. "And if you *do* make her happy, then that's the happiest you can be in this life."

In the dream the furry little monster has a birthday party, which is attended by other furry little monsters. We all sit around with party hats at a miniature tea table, the frame in which I view everybody like an old-fashioned black-and-white TV set. I'm simultaneously inside and outside the frame. Then somebody turns the TV set off, the screen goes black, and the monster is

in the room with me, smiling and asking for another piece of
birthday cake. I wake up in a cold sweat and look at Howard,
whose face is cast green in the light of the digital clock. I hear
a voice speaking on the other side of our bedroom door and
when I peep through the crack it's Darcy, having a conversation with herself. She is standing naked in the middle of the
living room, touching the tips of her fingers to her nose, as if
practicing for a police sobriety test.

"Isn't that right, Darcy?" she says, bending one elbow, then
the other.

"Oh, Darcy, but absolutely," she says, and squats down quickly, all the shadows in the room like jagged brushstrokes against
the skinny thighs, the dimpled ass, the braided stump of tail.

At the service bar the following morning Larry the bartender says, "Christine, honey, are you all right? You look like death
on a stick, Moonpie."

"I'm not sleeping well," I say. "And this job is tapping on
my last Christine nerve." I smile. Larry is a nice guy. He used
to come on to me, gave me the Moonpie nickname and everything, and then one day he stopped, I'm not sure why. I wouldn't
have done anything, I don't think, but I liked the energy. When
he turns to take another girl's order I look in the mirror behind
the bar: I'm skinny, and my breasts have gone down a full cup
size, but I still look like a thoroughbred at the gate. Nobody can
take that away from me.

I go back out onto the casino floor with the tray of drinks.
Some guy in the baccarat pit who gambles under the name of
John Q. Public propositions me behind his hand, three hun-
dred dollars for an hour in his room, "but hey, no rough stuff."
I'm not interested, though, and he catches an attitude with me,

dropping the hand from his face in a gesture of unconcealed disgust. "What, my money was good last week but bad this week? What? A skank like you should jump at the chance." I set the Scotch/rocks down on a paper napkin in front of him and stab the swizzle in. It's my job. The floorman and the dealer have heard the whole thing, so what? You pull the occasional trick, which in this town most women do, and next thing you're a card-carrying hooker?

A few days later it's Halloween and I put out a chip-n-dip in the shape of a pumpkin, guacamole, and silver coin margaritas. I've made these little tortillas in the shape of witches on broomsticks. I have a witch-on-her-broom tortilla mold. "The witch the witch!" I shriek. I have a witch joke only I never get to tell it. Whenever Darcy is around people never get to tell their witch jokes. You can't tell a witch joke properly when everybody only wants to sit there and look at Darcy. For her costume she's got on a silver vinyl slipdress and the velvet-rope gloves to the elbow. She's wearing a sign around her neck that says, "Friend of Karen Carpenter." Howard has the white bathrobe over his street clothes and a sign around his neck that says, "America's Guest." He should have a sign around his neck that says, "Christine's Guest."

In a minute Justin comes through the door in his plaid sportcoat, a pair of mirrored sunglasses, and a fake pencil mustache. He says, "Hi swingers!" He says, "Hi there, Howster!" He says, "Man, you're just *too* much!" He greets each of us as if he were an obnoxious gambler. He goes to kiss Martha on her cheek and she turns her head so that he catches her on the nose. Martha is on the couch next to Darcy. Martha is wearing this black leather outfit up to here, and Darcy has her hand on the inside of her thigh.

Justin is an Obnoxious Gambler, Darcy is Karen Carpenter's Friend, Howard is America's Guest. Martha doesn't seem to be anybody in particular. Myself, I'm Darcy. It was between Darcy and Paris Hilton. But I don't tell them I'm Darcy. When they ask me who I am, I tell them I'm Madonna. I thrust my tits out whenever I have something to say, and I twiddle my golden tresses, and I say, "I wanna fuck this *chair*. I wanna fuck this *table*. I mean, I wanna fuck *every*thing."

Darcy says, "I've never thought of Madonna the way you're doing her. You should be dancing around more. Or something."

"There isn't a guy in this town who wouldn't jump at the chance to eat my shorts!" I shriek, then punch Justin on the arm, one-two.

"Watch it," Justin says, "I'm friends with Moe Green."

For no good reason Justin sits down on the floor in front of the coffee table where Howard is cutting out the lines, and he takes off his shoes and socks. His little toe sits right on top of the one that is supposed to be next to it, piggyback. Everybody stares at it.

"I've asked you not to take your socks off in front of people," Martha says.

"That's like something atavistic," Darcy says.

"Like what?" Justin says.

"Put your socks on this minute!" Martha screams.

"You stick a sock in it," Justin laughs, and wiggles his freakish toes in front of her. "And what was it she just said about my toes?"

"Never mind about that now," Darcy says, holding out a

shiny chrome-plated pen. "Let me show you my latest innovation. The Space Pen. A pen that was designed for astronauts, men and women who have the right stuff. What would it be like to be stranded alone in outer space?" Darcy asks as if in voiceover. "And what, you may ask, *what* would it be like to be Karen Carpenter stranded in outer space?" She stands up on a kitchen chair and waves the pen around like a pointer in a planetarium. She writes HELP on the ceiling. Then she writes ME.

Howard and Martha fall out laughing.

Darcy sings "We've Only Just Begun."

The lines fly up off the glass, feathery pure.

On the radio is some cracker singing about how his baby done left him, and we drink margaritas until the sea-green feeling of alcohol gets mixed up with the sky-blue feeling of meth, still alert but all the emotions laid out on the surface like colored wires yanked from the back of a TV set.

"I had a witch joke to tell," I say. Everybody looks at me, but I can't remember the joke.

"Oh Christine," Howard whines, and he doesn't even finish the sentence.

Without another word I stand up and go through the kitchen out onto the fire escape, a pink patch of desert sky and the back ends of the apartments of all the people who are from someplace else, and I wonder where you go after you leave the place where all the people who are from someplace else are. I look down at a skinny dog tied up on a short piece of clothesline. I stand there smoking a cigarette. The sun showers the back of the Western Winds apartment complex, the tatty laundry and overflowing dumpsters, the labored *woof* of all the air conditioner compressors coughing hot air, and for a second it's like the whole world breaks down and rumbles to a halt. Slow figures of a caravan move like fingershadows across the pitted sky. A wooden flute plays a melody like a flock of sheep running over distant hills. Two girls in saffron robes whisper secrets behind pomegranate-stained hands. Then a door opens and I see Darcy and Martha, Justin bound at the ankles, his mouth taped shut, his wrists clamped to a steam pipe. *He wanted to watch us in action!* Martha cries. Then a door opens and I come into the apartment, Darcy kneeling at her brother's feet. *Hey baby*, Howard says. *Darcy here was just polishing my shoes.* Then a door opens and I'm in a hotel room with John Q. Public, I'm tired and naked and strung out but I need the money. *And I want you to keep smiling the whole time, skank, you hear me, I want you to—* Then a door opens and the furry little monster has a birthday party, which is attended by other furry little monsters. We all sit around with party hats at a miniature tea table, the frame in which I view everybody like an old-fashioned black-and-white TV set. I'm simultaneously inside and outside the frame. Somebody turns the TV set off, the screen goes blank, and the monster is in the room with me, smiling and asking for another piece of birthday cake. I wake up in a cold sweat and look at Howard, whose face is cast green in the light of the digital clock. I hear a voice speaking on the other side of our bedroom door and when I peep through the crack it's Darcy, having a conversation with herself. She's standing naked in the middle of the living room, touching the tips of her fingers to her nose, as if practicing for a police sobriety test.

"Isn't that right, Darcy?" she says, bending one elbow, then the other.

"Oh, Darcy, but absolutely," she says, and squats down quickly, all the shadows in the room like jagged brushstrokes against the skinny thighs, the dimpled ass, the braided stump of tail. When I open the door she stands up and I go to her. I touch her lips, stroke her tail. We sit together on the sofa, long into the night, the faintest brush of the hand or the flutter of an eyelash like something articulated for the first time, and it makes perfect sense to me that Darcy has a tail because when she touches me I have one too, and fur on my thighs soft as silk pajamas, and hooves of my own to *knock knock knock* against her own cleft feet.

Then a door opens and I'm out on the fire escape with Darcy, the sky in flames behind the blackened rooftops. The dog on its length of rope blinks, looks up at me, blinks again.

"Hey," Darcy says, and brushes the velvet-covered back of her hand against my arm, the side of my face, the ends of my hair.

"Hey," I say back. "Want to go someplace?" A look, something, the architecture of her face.

"Sure," Darcy says. "Where to?"

She takes her gloves off, one arm and then the other.

"Let's get lost," I say. "Let's just get *so* lost—"

The Unexamined Life

JACK HAD THE FURNITURE PULLED INTO THE center of his bedroom and covered with a canvas tarp. He put the roller dripping with black paint into the tray when he realized that Miles and Claire were standing just outside the open doorway.

"I've decided to redecorate," Jack said, leaning his elbow against an aluminum stepladder. "What do you think?"

"We can't leave you for five minutes," Claire said. "That's what I think."

"It's my room, right?" Jack asked. "I mean, am I right or am I right?" He was wearing white running shorts and a pair of black Doc Martens laced to the ankles, a bony kid with Claire's fine blond hair and blue-white skin, matte-black paint splotched on his face and hands.

"How about an explanation?" Miles said.

"It's like the Rolling Stones," Jack said. "They said to paint it black, so I did!"

"This goes back," Claire said. "This paint job definitely goes in reverse. Meanwhile, you can sit here and look at it."

Miles and Claire sat in the kitchen, having coffee. It was a large country kitchen and Claire had decorated it and the rest of the house in country colonial, gingham curtains and copper pots, a butter churn on the hearth, on the wall above the butcher-block table a brass sconce with a snowy scene of General Washington at Valley Forge painted on it. It was a good house—built in the twenties with wide-planked floors, high ceilings, and spacious rooms—left to Claire by a maiden aunt, photographs of whom she was beginning to resemble. The house sat tilted sideways on a piece of land that was once part of a blueberry farm; the lot was narrow across the front but went back a hundred yards into the pines. Late afternoon sunlight came trickling through the green-house windows that looked out on the ruined blueberry field.

"What are we going to *do*?" Claire wanted to know. She was smoking a cigarette and tapping her toes. She was wearing a faded pea-green summer shift and she seemed as if at any moment she might rocket out of it and land, stark naked, in the center of the room.

"We can wallpaper," Miles said.

"I'm serious, Miles. This is like demonology or something."

"It's not so bad, Claire," Miles said. "It's not the end of the world as we know it. I'll get some wallpaper and we'll wallpaper. It'll be good for him to learn how to wallpaper. We can redecorate his room the way he wants it. The three of us can do it together."

"Annie Roos has this kid they adopted from Korea," Claire said. "He's sixteen now and telling them he's going to set fire to them in their sleep. He has bad memories from Korea that nobody knew about. Now Annie and Mark have to sleep with their bedroom door locked. Is that the road you want to go down, Miles?"

"I'll take him fishing," Miles said. "Just the two of us."

Miles Dell worked as a craps dealer at the Circus Maximus Hotel-Casino. His dealer's uniform was a pair of plain black trousers and a white shirt embroidered at the collar and cuffs with golden Roman numerals and various arcane-looking and probably ersatz symbols. The cocktail waitresses wore white togas trimmed with the same pattern, and actors dressed as Caesar and Cleopatra strolled the casino floor reciting Shakespeare. The pit boss, a man from West Texas with overlarge ears, claimed to be dating Cleopatra.

"She's got stretch marks down to here," the pit boss said.

"Then why are you dating her?" the floorman asked.

"Because," the pit boss laughed, "the stretch marks are attached to the tits that are also down to here." He held out both hands and twirled the ends of his fingers.

"Strong," the floorman said.

"Double strong," the pit boss said.

At that moment the actress who played Cleopatra strolled by. She said, "I am dying, Egypt."

"Dying for some acting lessons," the floorman said.

The floorman, whose name was Guy Slater, was one of the few people Miles knew who actually seemed to have fun at this job; he approached the idea of being a completely useless member of society with tremendous gusto. He spent five days a week standing behind a craps table and talking to whoever would listen about the liberating aspects of horror and waste. Twenty years ago he'd gone to Williams College, where he'd studied English literature with a minor in classics. He said now, as he often said, "And then went down to the ship, set keel to breakers."

"And I'm the guy chained to the oar," Miles said, bending over to pay the pass line.

"Judah Miles Hur," Slater said.

"Three hundred dollars and I can't even get a decent meal," a customer complained.

Slater walked over to where the customer was standing in the space between the craps tables.

"Sir, yes sir, what is the problem, sir?"

The customer waved a comp slip in Slater's face.

"This is the problem," the customer said. He was old and bent sideways on an aluminum cane. "I ask you for dinner and you hand me this."

"Morris, don't make trouble," the customer's wife said.

"Stay out of it," the customer said.

"Sir," said Slater. "Relax, sir. This is the Circus Maximus family. You're a Circus Maximus family player, sir. And that is what I have to offer you today. That is the very best I can do and I assure you that it is a very nice sangwich indeed. Go up, you and your wife, set keel to breakers and have a nice corned beef sangwich. Have a beer and relax and live the life of real American people."

"A three-hundred-dollars corned beef sandwich," the customer said and limped away with the comp slip in his hand.

"Un sandweech de jambone," Slater said. He rubbed his palms together and gasped, "Dunt mayke trubble."

Slater was forty years old, four years younger than Miles, although he looked fifteen years younger. His black Armani suit fit him like a knifesheath. He drank and whored without apparent consequence or regret. He frequently told Miles that he knew what it meant to be alone in the world. He stood watching the costumed characters move up and down the cluttered aisles and frequently observed that they were standing on the trash heap of history, blades drawn.

"The Circus Maximus family," Slater said. "It's like the Von Trapp family, only different. The Nazis chase you into Switzerland and you end up in Vermont, running a ski lodge. You sing 'Edelweiss' for the people after they come back from a hard day on the slopes. You send a round of kirsch to the refugees at the corner table. Mein eyes have seen the glory!"

Slot machines clanked and rattled.

At the end of his shift Miles drove out of Atlantic City and down the long stretch of White Horse Pike with marshland on either side of it. The sun was still up, glinting on the tall grass, the bay at high tide tipping almost onto the narrow roadway. The ocean water shimmered like wrinkled foil and the salt air rushed into the blue Escort through both open windows. Two egrets stood pecking the dry grass. Miles pulled the car to the side of the road. After a while he started the engine and continued driving, but every few minutes he pulled over and stared out the window.

In the parking lot of the Absecon ShopRite he took off his dealer's shirt. Now he was just some guy in black pants and a plain white T-shirt. He drove west on the pike, and he had to put on his sunglass to cut the glare of the setting sun. He drove past Kennedy's Farm Market, the Ramshead Inn, the Lamplighter Motel, the American Legion Hall, the Bulldog Bar and Grill, the Renault Winery, est. 1865, Al's Original Smokehouse since 1975, Strike Zone Bowling, Red Barn Books, and the Harbor Diner. In twenty minutes he came to the stoplight where the pike intersected Philadelphia Avenue in Egg Harbor. Homeless men approached his car, hollering for change. Prostitutes walking the avenue half-naked propositioned him. Street boys soaped and smeared his windshield for fifty cents. On a whim he pulled into the McDonald's parking lot on the next corner, parked the car, and went into the restaurant.

He sat with his cheeseburger and fries, watching a family have dinner. The man took off his hat and said grace.

"Give us this day," the man said.

"As we forgive those," intoned the children.

The woman supervised the four children and the man sat as if by himself, staring at his meal in its paper wrappers. The children had names like Lisa Sue and John Bentley. Country people, Miles thought. Pineys.

After dinner he wandered Philadelphia Avenue. He went into a laundromat and sat quietly for fifteen minutes, watching the dryers turn. Next door to the laundromat was a tavern with a high cinderblock facade and a single small window with a red and green neon sign in it that said Joker Lounge. It was a Tuesday evening on the early side, and the narrow bar-room had six or seven people in it. Nobody looked up when he walked in and took a stool near the front door. The room was filled with cigarette smoke and was so dark that the few men and women present were just visible beneath the cloud cover. Behind the bar on a raised platform a girl with long black hair danced languidly around a brass pole. She was wearing a silver thong bathing suit and her breasts spilled out on either side of the skimpy material. The girl was dancing to a bluegrass num-ber with fiddles and mandolins, a man yodeling about a girl named Ruby who had driven him insane. A young couple at the other end of the bar did a quiet and incongruous two-step on the swept wooden floor. When the song was finished it started over again.

"That's that Holly Plish," an old woman behind the bar in-formed Miles. "She come in here and put three dollas in the juke and we hear for a hour about how Ruby driven that man to be insane. What'll you have?"

"Draft beer." Miles reached into his pants pocket and set a creased five dollar bill on the bartop.

The woman drew the beer and put the change next to it, three ones and four quarters. "Beer's a dolla because the dancer is on," the old woman said.

"Sure."

She slid a basket heaped with broken pretzels next to the glass of beer.

"On the house," she said, and made no move to go. She was short, with a tight bun of gray hair twisted onto the very top of her head and large breasts that ballooned under her loose housedress as if stirred by a slight but sudden breeze.

"I never seen you," the old woman said.

"That makes us even," Miles said.

"You're a big strappin' fella," she said, and winked. "Name's Agnes Kogod."

"John Bentley," Miles told her. He had never considered giving anyone anything but his real name before that moment, but it seemed the right thing to do. He was not in a place where he belonged or where he could trust anyone. Nevertheless, he looked past Agnes into the glass above the whiskey bottles and came to the conclusion that he didn't look entirely out of place, either. His slack, ruddy face and plain white T-shirt and big arms all seemed to fit with the surroundings.

"Rules are as follows," Agnes Kogod said. "Don't touch the girls and don't talk dirty to the girls. Don't proposition the girls and don't expect anything out of them. Any of my girls mix in with the customers I fire 'em like a shot."

Miles drained the glass of beer in two long swallows and added, "But I see only one girl."

"You're a smartmouth, John Bentley," Agnes said, and scowled. Then she laughed, exhaling simultaneously through both sides of her mouth, and punched him good-naturedly on the arm. She grabbed both his forearms and he could see her breasts straining and billowing against her open dressfront. She pressed her face inches from his and stuck out her tongue like a blackened bit of sausage.

"You want to play then let's play," Agnes Kogod said.

"Maybe later."

Agnes stepped back and released his arms and refilled the beer glass and set up a shot of sour mash next to it. The voice coming from the jukebox yodeled, "Ru-beee—!" The girl danced around the pole, one leg up and then thrust straight out as she spun.

"I've got a wedding ring," Miles said.

"Any one of them worth bothering about has got a wedding ring," Agnes said. She trilled, "Married John Bentley—with the ladies goes gently!"

"Well."

"Dontchu?" Agnes barked. "Dontchu?"

"I guess I do."

"You know you do." A customer hollered for beer and Agnes instructed him to blow it out his ass. The door opened and a short blast of hot air rushed into the bar. A small girl with spiky, purplish-red hair sat down on the stool next to Miles. She had on a tight pair of jeans, torn not very stylishly, and a lipstick-red halter top.

"The bad seed," Agnes said, looking at the girl. "This girl had a good job here but she had to get greedy," Agnes said, turning to Miles. "I fired her like a shot. I sent her down to Uncle Billy's finishing school to learn her some manners. How's life among the whips and chains?" Agnes asked the girl.

"I can't even come in here and get a quiet glass of beer," the girl said. "I take shit all day from him and now I got to come in here and take shit from you."

"You don't have to come in here at all," Agnes said. "Nobody ast you to."

She drew a beer and set it down without a coaster in front of the girl.

"There's a beer," Agnes said. "Nice and quiet. You listen to it, it won't make a sound. She had it good in here, little Patsy did, but she ruined things for herself," Agnes said to Miles. "She's always ruining things for herself, little Patsy is. But there's one in every family I guess."

"I guess there is," Miles said. He knocked back the shot, finished the beer, and plucked up a few pretzels for the road.

"Come on back when you can stay awhile, John Bentley," Agnes called after him. "You come on back now. You hear?"

Patsy finished her beer in a long swallow that overflowed her small mouth and ran down her shirtfront. She followed Miles out onto the pavement. She said: "Listen mister, I'm a little short and I'll do you for forty dollars in your car. No time to beat around the bush with a fast-walker like you."

"Maybe next time."

"I like you, mister," Patsy said. "I like big guys. I wouldn't do nobody for money I wouldn't do for free."

"Then why charge me?"

"I got bills to meet, baby. And nothing in this life is free. You pay me the money means you don't have to hear my female bullshit. And you'll like it, I'm telling you. You want to save some money you go back home right now, because you're gonna be back for it every night once you get a little taste a heaven!"

"That's a nice line," Miles said. "You're a real pro, I guess."

"Oh," Patsy said. "You haven't got no idea."

They came to his car in the McDonald's parking lot and stood in front of it.

"That's a nice car," Patsy said.

"It's an eight-year-old Escort," Miles said. "The right front quarter panel is held on with duct tape."

"I was named for Patsy Cline the greatest female vocalist in country music," Patsy said. "I've sang in bar bands and I've been told I'm not half bad."

Miles wondered what that had to do with the right front quarter panel, or anything else, for that matter, but obviously it did have to do with something because he unlocked the passenger side for her. He pulled the car to the very back of the lot, next to the dumpster where the streetlight was out. He handed her two twenties that disappeared the second they hit the air. He touched his fingertips to the downy place at the nape of her neck and said, "Honeybaby."

"Come and see my act over at Uncle Billy's," Patsy said, one knuckle turned sideways into the corner of her mouth, the door already open. "Come watch me work sometime. I go on, every day, two o'clock sharp, give or take an hour." She got out without closing the door behind her and skipped away in the direction of the littered avenue.

"Where've you been?" Claire asked, standing behind the front door. "I was getting worried." It was seven-thirty and daylight was failing at the very tops of the trees at the back of the property, a short steady signal of light, opalescent, like a tiny nuclear explosion.

"I got a flat tire," Miles answered. He held up the palms of his hands as if to show that they were covered with grease, then moved quickly into the house through the living room and into the kitchen.

"You're soaking *wet*," Claire said, pressing the palm of her hand to the small of his back.

"You try changing a tire in this heat."

"I'll get dinner started while you change." Claire paused for a moment, watching.

"What? What is it?"

"Something," Claire said. "I don't know. Something about you."

"I just told you—"

"Yeah, I know, the flat tire," Claire said, turning to the stove. "Men always come home covered with slime and shaking uncontrollably after they've changed a flat tire."

"I'm not—" He trailed the sentence off and left the room. He showered and shaved, put on a pair of jeans and a white polo shirt with a red and black penguin stitched into the breast pocket.

He stopped at Jack's room but the door was closed, the lights turned off, the sound of a record that played as if stuck in its groove: "All I wanna do is—all I wanna do is—all I wanna do is—boom boom—"

"Well," said Claire when he came back into the kitchen. And that was all she said. Together they ate a dinner of spaghetti and meatballs with a loaf of Italian bread from the Hammonton bakery. Miles had a glass of red wine, a second, a third. The day began to lose its edge and as the heat died down a short breeze kicked up. The cicadas buzzed in the fields and trees all around them like the defective buzzing of a florescent lightbulb. After-

ward they sat out in their rocking chairs, just the two of them,
the evening breeze slanting sideways down the narrow covered porch.

"Golf," Claire said.

"Huh? What was that?"

"It's how I'll save him. Golf."

In the morning Jack began to act out the terms of his punish-
ment, clearing and leveling the old aunt's ruined blueberry
patch into a shag field where he could practice his drive.
Claire's father was a scratch golfer even now, and Claire considered golf the key to right conduct in America. Miles watched
Jack through the kitchen window, considering that it wasn't
the worst way the kid could spend his time. He hacked his way
in a straight line away from the house with a small scythe, the
handle and shaft of which had been fashioned to replicate a
golf club. He took his time, and his form was very good. When
the heat rose toward midday he came back inside the house
and showered and then stood in the kitchen, toweling off his
hair while Claire fixed a lunch suspiciously festive for a Tuesday afternoon.

"Let's go fishing," Miles said to Jack after lunch. "Can he get
out of jail to go fishing for a few hours?" Miles said to Claire.

"You're the man," Claire said, washing dishes. "He can do
whatever you say he can do."

"We'll pick some huckleberries for a pie," Miles offered. "I
was walking out by the pond last week and they're growing fat
as blueberries."

"I'll start rolling out the crust this minute," Claire said without apparent irony.

Jack grinned and the corner of his mouth quivered slightly.

Running behind the back of the property was a utility road that led to a pond where Miles fished with a barbless hook for carp, bluegills, and largemouth bass. He liked to feel the fish hit the line, the jerk and sputter at the tip of the rod. He liked to set the hook and feel the desperate thrash on the other end. He always brought the fish in slowly, then gently removed the hook, holding the fish with wet hands so as not to damage the scales and let in disease. His favorite part was to watch the fish swim away.

"We'll get bitten by ticks and get Lyme disease and suffer paralysis and short-term memory loss," Jack said, trooping along just ahead of Miles. "We'll develop flulike symptoms. We'll have a spot on us that looks like a bull's eye."

"It's possible."

"Why do we want to catch fish anyway?" Jack asked. "We never eat them."

"It's fun, I think."

"Not for the fish," Jack said.

"Everybody's got to have it tough once in a while," Miles offered.

"That's us," Jack said. "Spreaders of good cheer."

"Plus we have to get the huckleberries," Miles said.

"Let's tell her all the huckleberry trees are dead," Jack laughed. "Let's tell her the locusts ate them up."

"You have an evil mind, kiddo."

"I'm working on it," Jack said. "And what's up with these locusts, anyway?"

"They come out of the ground, lay their eggs, and die. The young ones go back into the ground for seven more years. Then they do it all over again."

"So they stay awake for, like, two weeks?"

"I guess so."

"That's extra stupid."

"It must serve some purpose. Who knows what?"

The trees and the cars and the sides of houses were covered with locusts. They looked like grasshoppers only with broader backs and shorter legs, a brown line running down the center of the Kelly-green topshell where the wings folded together. Miles caught one in his fingertips and spliced a hook through its belly and cast it out on the stagnant green water. Jack jammed a ball of dough onto his hook and lobbed it a few yards. The sinker took it straight to the bottom.

"Bass in this pond," Miles told Jack. "I've see them rise in the spring. They're down deep now, cooling on the bottom. Let's see if one rises to the bait."

"Wickity-whack," Jack said.

"So what about your room?" Miles asked. "There's more to this than the Rolling Stones."

"Black is the color of my true love's hair," Jack said.

The tip of Jack's pole began to twitch. He pulled back and stood up and the fish on the other end began to peel off line.

"Tighten the drag," Miles said.

"DA-HAH," Jack said. He tightened up a bit and jerked a small ugly fish onto the sand, a black and white mottled carp, its flesh peeled away in places like old wallpaper. Miles put his own pole down and squatted to wet his hands. The hook was deep in the fish's gullet, and he had to reach in with a pair of needle-nose pliers to extract it.

"I'm sorry," Miles said. "I'm sorry to hurt you."

The fish rolled and flopped in the sand and blood spurted from its open mouth. Miles held the fish down with one hand

and twisted the pliers with the other; the hook came loose, along with part of the fish's entrails. Miles stood up, holding the pliers and the bare hook. Jack smashed the fish under the heel of his shoe. He twisted his mouth up and looked as if he was going to cry. He scraped the bottom of his shoe against a rock and walked away, throwing his arms in the air.

Miles packed up the gear and trudged back to the house.

Beside the kitchen door Claire was spraying white powder on a trellised rose bush.

Uncle Billy's porn shop was set out on a bend of the White Horse Pike between two farm stands. Facing the road on one side of the door was a nine-foot photograph of a whip-wielding dominatrix laminated to a buckled piece of plywood, on the other side a similarly mounted photo of a girl on her hands and knees, bound at the ankles, cuffed at the wrists, a red ball plugged into her open mouth. At the center, above the aluminum door, was a sign that said, "Uncle Billy's." A hand-painted caricature of a balding, avuncular man in suspenders smiled beneficently downward.

Three motorcycles were cut into the space of gravel beneath the submissive girl; they were large, immaculate, expensive looking. A paper sign on the smeared doorglass said, "Push Hard." Miles pushed through the door that asked to be pushed hard. Uncle Billy, unmistakably, was standing high up at the counter in front of a small oscillating fan. He gazed into it as into a mirror. The front of the shop was occupied by three bikers who picked their way among the cluttered aisles like a band of foraging bears.

"Here's one," a tall, skinny boy said. "*Gang Bang.*"

"We already seen that one," said another.

"We see that one every night," laughed the fat bearded one. Then all three laughed.

Uncle Billy said to Miles, "What you want?" The fan rustled the hairs that sprouted like brittle weeds from the top of his skull.

"I want to see the show."

"You want to see the show?" Uncle Billy said, pointing a finger toward the purple curtain above which a sign said, Live Show. Taped to the wall was a piece of red construction paper on which was printed in childish block letters: *Only one person at one time in the booths. Violators will be bared for life.*

Miles pushed through the purple drapery, trying his best not to touch anything. A long hallway confronted him. On the right side the paneled wall seemed solid, on the left there were small lights, like nightlights, above a row of curtained booths that reminded him of the booths they used to have in penny arcades to take your picture, three for a quarter. He stopped for a moment to listen to the low grunting sounds of the men in the booths. The end booth, curtain drawn back, was vacant. The wooden floor was tacky and the soles of his shoes stuck to it. He edged in sideways and sat down with his hands on his knees. He opened his wallet and fed a ten dollar bill into the slot and a black screen dropped down. Patsy Kogod was in the room on the other side of the glass. She stood tilted forward on a pair of spiked heels so high and slender they wobbled, and she was draped in an ill-fitting leather costume, as if she'd recently replaced a larger employee. The outfit was done up with black fishnet at the exposed midriff, leather shorts and fishnet stockings, a dog collar with silver studs and a large eyebolt at the base of Patsy's skull. You could easily see the collar from behind because her magenta-colored hair was cut short and twisted into jagged points on top.

Miles looked at her narrow back, her rickety bowed legs. Above his head a red bulb flashed on. A voice from somewhere inside the booth informed him that the girl he was looking at wanted him desperately. She was hungry for his throbbing member; she was thirsty for some cum-quenching action. Miles laughed, even as he realized he had an erection. The black screen fell and he put another ten into the changer and the screen jerked up again. The girl on the other side of the glass removed her top; she licked her chapped lips in a not very convincing manner. The voice informed Miles that he could do whatever he felt like doing to the girl. At the same time, she turned languidly to reveal a scarred back, the vertebrae clearly visible beneath the parchment-colored skin. On either shoulder a flurry of welts rose up like a fresh case of measles. The voice told Miles that the girl wanted to be fucked and beaten. She was bad, that was what she deserved. Only a man like Miles could hurt her in just the right way. So that it was good. So that she would be good. The girl wanted to be good, the voice said. She just didn't know how. She needed a man like Miles, a firm hand. At this a man in a black leather mask came into the room. He was naked from the waist up and carried with him a leather whip and a conventional dog's leash, a thin chrome chain attached to a droopy yellow handgrip. The screen dropped and Miles exited the booth before the first lash of the whip came down.

"How'd you like the show?" Uncle Billy asked.

"It was good," Miles said, moving toward the door. "It was very well done."

"Well shit fuck piss!" declared Uncle Billy.

The narrow country road cut through the scorched pine forest. Many of the mailboxes in front of the ranch homes and trailers had the name Kogod stenciled or scrawled on them, as if the place itself might be called Kogod. Patsy's house sat not even twenty feet from the road, a red bungalow on an unlevel cinderblock foundation around which no shrubs had been planted. Miles tapped the back of his hand on the screen door frame.

"Hey there John Bentley," Patsy said, coming into dark, blurry focus on the other side of it. "How you making?"

"I wanted to see you."

"You know where I work at. How'd you find me?"

"I wanted to see you outside of work."

"It's a hundred dollars," Patsy said. "I have a kid in here. It's a hundred dollars. All right? How'd you find me? It's a hundred dollars. How'd you *find* me?"

"I followed you."

A small TV flickered in the cramped living room. A little girl with feathery blond hair sat cross-legged on the greenish-black shag carpet, staring at it.

Patsy turned and went into the bedroom and Miles followed after her. He looked over his shoulder. The little girl was still staring at the TV set. Patsy was taking off her clothes. She pulled the clothes from Miles, and they fell together into the unmade bed. "Get in," Patsy said. Miles thought she was talking to him, but she was talking to the little girl who was standing in the open doorway. Miles looked at the little girl and she went away. He pressed his face into the hollow of Patsy's collarbone and came in a few short strokes.

"Your daughter?" Miles asked, sitting up. "Your little girl?"

"My ball and chain."

"She seems all right to me."

"You can't get her," Patsy said, and whipped her head from side to side. "I don't allow that. You can go again if you want to but that's it, a hundred bucks. But you can't get her. I don't allow that. You want head this time? What you want?"

"That's all right. That was enough."

Patsy laughed. "Come again. Any time." Then, "You want her? How much?"

"No, I don't want her."

"You and me both."

She had a giggling fit, stood up and walked around the room picking up things while Miles put on his clothes. He gave her the hundred dollars and went out. At the door Patsy said, "Don't tell Uncle Billy you were over here. Don't tell Billy. You come back any time but just don't you tell Billy."

"I won't tell anybody," Miles promised. "My lips are sealed."

"You're sweet. Next time I'll show you a better time. Come back again and I'll really get you going. I was tired tonight. You liked it all right?"

"I liked it fine."

Patsy giggled. "You're easy, mister," she said. "You're too damn easy." She stood just inside the threshold and her robe fell open and her small pale breasts spilled out. The little girl crawled in the open space between her mother's legs.

"You and me both."

Miles got into his car and went home. He sat by himself in the kitchen, drinking beer out of the bottle. Outside the window he could hear the rhythmic *pok* of driven golf balls.

"Seven out, take the line!" the stickman hollered.

Miles reached out to pick up the chips on the pass line. He straightened his back and groaned; his feet were killing him, his sciatic nerve screaming down the back of his left leg. At the center of the table sat an old man, counting money. His name was David Mackie, and he'd been sitting behind a craps table for most of the past forty years. He claimed to have worked for Bugsy Siegel at the Flamingo and to have killed a man in a barfight, in self-defense, followed by five years in Joliet. Miles wondered how you committed a crime in Nevada and ended up in prison in Illinois, but he never asked about it. It was a story, probably, the way most people in this place had stories, some of them true, some of them less than true, a way to pass the time, to make life more interesting.

David Mackie looked up at Miles and said: "When you can no longer stand up then you must sit down."

He sang an ancient shanty about Jonah in the belly of the whale. He droned chorus after chorus above the clang and ping of slot machines, bets called out, money won and money lost.

"I am dying, Egypt," Cleo said.

"Well then drop dead already," Slater said.

"They will fire us hence like foxes," Caesar said.

"Life in the postmodern," Slater said. "You never know which century you're standing in around here. Ah, well," Slater said. "Forth on the godly sea."

The two men went on break together and sat in the employees' cafeteria, drinking coffee from Styrofoam cups.

"I'm having an affair," Miles said to Slater. "I'm seeing someone."

"Yeah, so?" Slater asked. "Want a medal?"

"Well, aren't you just a little surprised?"

"Why should I be? It's about time you wised up. I'm happy to think I may have been a good influence on you, in a negative sort of way."

"I'm in it but I'm not happy about it," Miles said. "I want to stop."

"These things run their course soon enough," Slater said. "Sit back and enjoy it while you can. Does Claire know?"

"I don't think she has any idea. I'd be surprised."

"Then you're living. Listen, Miles, don't be dopey. You work hard and pull the plow here in good old bag-over-head America. Does it hurt anything very much if you take the bag off once in a while? Breathe the clean fresh air and lead the clean good life of a real American person? I hate to say it, big fella, but you're a bit of a stiff. I mean, who does everything they're supposed to do except a chump? It's a sign your life is unexamined. And you know what they say about the unexamined life?"

"What?"

"Well, don't let me be the one to break the news to you, then. But I will say this: if you looked into your own heart once in a while you'd see how scared and lonely you are, what a big fat failure you've made of your life. Fifteen years ago, perhaps, you thought you'd go back to school, change jobs, maybe even fall in love again. But you didn't. What you have in front of you is pretty much what you're stuck with. Face up to that, my friend, and the fun can begin! I'd like to get married, actually, just so I could fool around. And the girls eat it up, getting something they're not supposed to have. I cruise the bars once in a while with a wedding band on and you wouldn't believe how well I do."

"You actually tell women you're married when you're not?"

"Sure, why not? They like it, and it keeps them off my back in the long term."

"Talking to you is like talking to the devil in a cheap suit," Miles said.

"Watch it," Slater said. "This suit cost eight hundred dollars."

"I can't stop thinking about her," Miles said.

"Try phone sex," Slater said. "Did you ever try phone sex? It's great. Cost you an arm and a leg, though."

"I don't think I could with Claire in the house. Seems a bit demeaning, anyway."

"Most of life as a so-called sentient being is demeaning," Slater said, lighting a cigarette.

"This is the no smoking section," Miles said.

"I find no smoking sections *highly* demeaning."

Miles stood fishing in the still afternoon. He cast a hand-painted plug that had been his father's out toward the middle of the algae-covered pond. He jerked the tip of the pole and the plug popped and wriggled to simulate a wounded minnow. The green day hummed all around him. The sound of locusts echoed off the trees, a shimmery sound that went on and on. Jack came up the path from the house, pulling a teenage girl by the tips of her fingers.

"This is Alison Six," Jack said.

"Hello, Miss Six," Miles said.

"Call me Alison," Alison Six said.

She stood in front of Miles, flexing the tips of her fingers. She was thin and blond, done up in tight black clothes, silver bangles at her wrists and throat.

"I just came back from a trip with my church group," Alison Six said. "We went to help relieve the coal miners of Kentucky."

"And how are the coal miners of Kentucky?"

"Poor," Alison Six said. "And not very clean."

"What did you do down there?"

"We baked brownies and prayed a lot. It was all right. I'm glad I'm not a miner of coal in Kentucky, though. You can have that. I was thinking about doing missionary work, but if you land in a place like that I mean, let's be real."

"Yes," Miles said. "Let's be real. That's what I want, too."

"That's right." Alison Six looked at Miles. She blinked her eyes and did a little pirouette on the tips of her shoes.

"Come on," Jack said, taking her by the hand. "Let him get a girlfriend of his own."

"Who says I'm anybody's girlfriend?" Alison Six wanted to know.

"It's been years since I baked a huckleberry pie," Claire said to Miles. She rinsed the huckleberries Miles had picked on his way back from the pond.

"I bought a new pie basket and I want to try it out. We can take it to my parents' house. We're having dinner with them Friday night."

"Can I ask what exactly *is* a pie basket?"

"It's a basket that you carry your pie in."

"Why would you need a pie basket, Claire?"

"I already answered that question once, but if you must. You need a pie basket to carry your pie in because if you don't then it sloshes around on the floor of the car. Maybe the crust breaks. Maybe it's still a little warm and you wouldn't want it on your lap, especially in August in a car that has no air conditioning. And the basket is ventilated, so the pie can cool while you carry it along with you. Look here."

Claire brought out a wicker basket that looked like a picnic basket with little plastic sunflowers twisted into the handle and green ribbon patterned with tiny sunflowers stitched around the lid.

"See?" Claire said, opening the basket. "There's a well in the basket where a twelve-inch pie plate can sit, snug as a bug." She beamed.

"It's just lovely," Miles said, and lumbered off into the paneled living room.

Patsy Kogod jabbed the point of a syringe into the grainy, porous flesh behind her knee. She was thin and sickly as a child: corpse-white skin, vacant smile, butch-cut hair the color of strawberry pie. Her mouth went all gluey, then she lit a cigarette and got expansive.

"Uncle Billy came after me when I was twelve and a half," Patsy said to Miles, "and he ain't never let up since then. One time I seen him chew the head off a live squirrel."

She took her top off and turned her back to Miles.

"He like to burn me with his cigarettes," Patsy said. "He like that more than anything on this earth, to burn me. And I let him. I let him do it. I don't know no other way how to be."

"You could say no," Miles said.

"No I can't," Patsy said.

Miles grabbed the cigarette from her. He took both of her wrists in one hand and touched the cigarette to her back with the other.

"That's extra," Patsy said as Miles pushed the smoking cigarette into her shoulder. "You can do it but it's extra."

"Bill me," Miles said. He lost himself in the sour scent at the nape of her neck, the disorder of the room, the last fat motes of daylight spinning off the tall trees in the space just beyond the blinded window. He peeled the condom off in the middle of it and knew he'd crossed a line. What was it like here on the other side where people just did whatever came to mind, lust and squalor and hopelessness like the dark shaft of a centerpole in a tent where all the lights had been extinguished, night vision, shadows and silvery shapes as they rose and fell, everything in the world reduced to seeming, down and down. He slapped mindlessly at her as she seemed for a moment to disappear and then reappear; she cried out and stiffened at the hips and he held to her, two bony points like the spoke-ends of a wheel. He had a momentary urge to break one of her arms but resisted it.

Afterward Patsy lay sleeping. Miles dressed, closed the bedroom door behind him, sat for a while in the dank, cluttered living room. The little girl, whose name was Stevie, crawled across his lap. He held her up in front of him. She was heavy, solid.

"You're a dirty, smelly little girl," Miles said. She stared back at him with luminous black pupils.

Miles gave little Stevie a bath and while she soaked he told her the story of a floating plastic bunnyrabbit that wished he was a goldfish. When she was clean and dry he covered her in an oversized Susie Brite T-shirt, then took her into the kitchen and fixed her some supper, tomato soup with little goldfish crackers that wished they were bunnyrabbits. He had some himself, washed the dishes, and went home.

"Let's go to Nova Scotia next summer," Claire said to Miles at dinner. Jack was out somewhere with Alison Six and it was just the two of them, Miles tripping over himself to be solicitous. "Let's go up there and eat lox and Canadian bagels for a week."

"Sounds good," Miles said. "Do we need to bring our own cream cheese?"

"Probably. But maybe they have a Canadian way to eat it. We can drive up the coast and get this overnight ferry in Bar

Harbor. I've been reading about it. Even Jack will want to go,
I bet."

"Maybe Alison Six will want to tag along."

"You sure know how to wreck a mom's good time," Claire
said.

Miles went into the refrigerator and opened a beer. The
house was quiet. The appliances hummed in a way that pleased
him. This was his. Why did he have to go and throw it all away?
That was the question, wasn't it? Yes, that was the question that,
if you gave the right answer, they paid you all the money.

"I am telling you, my friend, that you are there for one reason
and one reason only," Slater said, exhaling cigarette smoke.
"You do not go to a plumber expecting to purchase a diamond
ring, neither do you employ a carpet-cleaning service to install
a new roof."

"This isn't the Yellow Pages," Miles said.

"Maybe it ought to be," Slater added. "If you're about to do
what I think you're about to do then maybe somebody should
tell you to run on home, your mamma's calling you." Slater
looked at Miles, blinked, puffed his cigarette. "Remember Oe-
dipus?" Slater asked, but Miles didn't remember any such person. "He thought he was in one place, over here," and Slater put
his right hand on the smeary cafeteria tabletop. "But it turned
out he was really all the way over *here*." Slater extended his
left arm, and the manicured fingers on the end of it dangled in
empty space.

"Do you love Alison Six?" Miles asked Jack. He stood in the center of Jack's bedroom, tapping a golfball in and out of a plastic
cup.

"What kind of question is that?" Jack wanted to know.

"I thought you liked questions," Miles said, glancing at the wallpaper that Claire had chosen to cover the black paint. Red and gold question marks the size of dollar bills, some of them upended, floated in a vibrant field of blue. "I'm not against asking the tough questions," Claire had explained. "I never said that."

"I'm just curious," Miles said. "It's about time you fell in love. Everybody does, you know. Oftentimes not to their overwhelming advantage."

"I guess I do," Jack said. "Except that she's a gigantic pain in the ass some of the time, I think she's—excellent."

"I suppose she is pretty excellent," Miles said.

"She's not like anybody I ever met."

"You're a goner," Miles said, handing Jack the club. "Want to play some golf?"

"Want to jab a pointy stick in my eye?" asked Jack.

After high school Miles worked at the Sears out at the Shore Mall during the time when the entire mall had been called Searstown. Miles worked in sporting goods and after a few years moved up to manager of the department. Nobody else seemed to stay around long enough to become manager, so finally Miles became manager. That was in 1978, and the job of manager of the sporting goods department of Sears paid $16,400. It wasn't terrible money for the time but it wasn't so great, either. And where could he go from manager of sporting goods? The general manager was not going anywhere and frequently said so.

Later that spring Resorts International opened the first hotel-casino in Atlantic City, and stories began to circulate about people who, with a little training, were making a thousand dollars a week. In the evening Miles attended the Rum Point School of Gaming to learn how to deal craps, and at Rum Point he met Claire, who was at that time also a few years out of high school and learning how to deal blackjack. They began to date, talking of their future careers in the casino business, the money they would earn and also the glamour of it, perhaps even the chance to travel. It seemed an adventurous way to avoid the ordinary, boring nine-to-five life most people seemed fated for.

A little later though, when they landed their first casino jobs, they realized pretty quickly that it was not so different from factory work. In the meantime, and on the strength of the money they were bringing in, Miles and Claire got married and then a year later the old aunt left Claire the house in Hammonton. Jack came along a few years later and Miles told Claire to quit her job dealing blackjack, she could be a full-time mother and they could live off the money Miles was making as a craps dealer at the Circus Maximus, not a thousand a week but not so shabby for a high school graduate. As time went on the opportunity for small promotions came up, the industry was so new and the positions in lower management jobs so plentiful that you didn't have to be very aggressive or even very bright: you only had to deal the number of hours required by the State of New Jersey to get the upgrade to floorperson or boxperson on your gaming license, following which you could spend your days sitting at a craps table instead of standing at one. Miles didn't take these promotions as they were offered, though, because he didn't want to give up his days off—Sunday/Monday, very desirable and almost impossible to replace once given up—and he didn't want to be sent to swing shift for three or four years, missing all those evenings with his family and closing up craps tables at three o'clock in the morning. He didn't mind doing this kind of work but he wanted a normal family life. And he was old enough by now to know that in life there is always a tradeoff. He accepted the tradeoff, or thought he did.

He remained a casino dealer, standing five days a week behind a craps table, pushing the chips around for eight or nine hours, inhaling secondhand cigar and cigarette smoke, eating the not really terrible food in the employee cafeteria on his breaks, driving to and from work, years and years to travel in a hearse-like black Olds 98 Claire's father had given them as a wedding present, which was in time replaced by a blue Ford Escort, up and down the White Horse Pike.

Howard Johnson's
U-Haul
Absecon ShopRite
Kennedy's Farm Market
The Ramshead Inn
The Lamplighter Motel
The American Legion Hall
The Bulldog Bar and Grill
The Renault Winery, est. 1865
Al's Original Smokehouse since 1975
Strike Zone Bowling
Red Barn Books
Uncle Billy's
Harbor Diner
Last Resort Bar and Grill
A sign that says -----------Markets

Angelo's Farm Market
Various casino billboards, including a smiling, wooly-
    haired cartoon character called Sling-O who is depict-
    ed as both angel and demon
Bali Hai Tavern and Tiki Bar
Porky's Point
Green Thumb Gardening
Columbia Restaurant (now taking New Year's Eve
    reservations)
Mullica Mobile Manor
Axeactly Music Store
Fireside Steakhouse
City of Hammonton, America's Blueberry Capital!

When Miles thought about his life in this way he realized that
it was a fairly drastic oversimplification, but he didn't have
any other way to think about it. His life certainly wasn't what
he'd expected, but he also knew that things were not as dire as
they seemed when he tried to describe his life to himself while
lying awake at three o'clock in the morning. After all, he and
Claire had had some good times, had been a real couple at one
time if they weren't so close these days, and Jack seemed to be
turning out to be a good kid and a pretty smart one, too. There
were other ways of looking at this; in fact, there were a lot of
other ways of looking at this. In fact, there were so many ways
of looking at this that when he was finished he always felt he'd
landed back exactly where he started.

   Thinking his life through—examining it, as Slater would
say—was exactly like driving up and down the White Horse
Pike in a blue Ford Escort. Miles lay in bed, staring at the full

moon until the faintest bit of daylight began to leak onto the space of pea-colored carpet at the foot of the bed.

"You can't come back," Claire said. She was wearing an apron the straps of which were embroidered with yellow tea roses, her face and hands smudged with pastry flour.

He thought of Claire, back when they were first dating. He'd been awkward, shy. She'd taken charge right away, told him what to do, what she liked, what she didn't. He'd appreciated that, because on his own he'd have had absolutely no idea. Claire hadn't changed all that much, it occurred to him.

"No. I know that," he answered. It was his decision. "I'm sorry, Claire."

"Oh, Miles," Claire said. She took the dough from the floured board and held it up in front of her. "The world's a rotten place."

Miles drove the winding country road, imagining what would what happen next. He could see the brick-red bungalow, the brown rectangle of grass, the house tilted sideways on its cracked foundation. The rusted mailbox with its red flag, marking the turn in the road.

"I can't keep away from you," Miles said, the screen door swinging loosely on its splintered frame.

"I'm a regular Sharon Stone, I guess."

They stood facing one another in the cluttered living room. Patsy was dressed for work. Miles stepped forward and grabbed her by the dog collar, which he unbuckled and let fall to the floor.

"I love you," Miles said.

Patsy blinked hard and clutched at herself as if a chill had just run through her. She blinked again and looked down at the soiled space of carpet where the dog collar lay. She kicked it with the pointed tips of her boots. Little Stevie crawled up and sat down on the tops of Miles's shoes.

"You can quit that now," Miles said. "I'm here. I can take care of you. I can save you."

Patsy walked into the bedroom, smiled wanly and sat down with her hands pressed between her knees. Miles picked up little Stevie and hefted her backwards over his right shoulder. Her clothing was sticky and she smelled bad. She tangled her fingers in his hair; she made tiny gurgling sounds in his ear. He grabbed up both ankles in his left hand. She'd need a bath, Miles thought, and some dinner.

"Time for a visit with Mr. Bunnyrabbit," Miles whispered, closing his eyes for just a moment, and when he opened them he was in exactly the place he always thought he'd be: red lop-sided bungalow, woman and child, dented mailbox to mark the turn in the road, in the front yard turned sideways in a wash of sand and gravel a blue Ford Escort to take him wherever in the world he wanted to go.

The Burnie-Can

I N THE EARLY SUMMER OF 1966 MY GRAND-
mother captured a baby dinosaur, or maybe it was a fully
grown dinosaur, just a small one. She trapped it under a
clothes basket. It was early in the afternoon, just after lunch,
and she and my mother were the only two people at home. It
was a hot July day. My sister Ailie and I were off swimming at a
nearby lake. My father and grandfather were both at their jobs,
down at the Owens-Corning plant, working on their asbesto-
sis. When the dinosaur arrived my grandmother was out in the
backyard, taking laundry down off the line and folding it into a
red plastic clothes basket. My mother was in the house, chain-
smoking cigarettes and watching *Days of Our Lives*.

We all heard about it over dinner, and even though it was
my grandmother who'd caught the dinosaur, it was my mother
who began to tell the story, and I think the four of us who hadn't
been there probably chalked the whole thing up to my mother's fondness for diet pills. In fact, there was a copy of *Reader's
Digest* out in the living room with an article that my sister had
urged my mother to read. The title of the article was "The Diet
Pill Menace."

"I was in the house," my mother explained. "Nan was outside, folding the sheets. Then she came into the living room
and said, 'I trapped a dinosaur under the clothes basket. Hurry
up! I trapped a dinosaur under the clothes basket!'"

But when they lifted the clothes basket up the dinosaur ran away. Up to this point my mother told the story, and then they both began speaking at the same time, breaking in on each other's account of what the creature looked like and what had happened next.

"He was like a lizard but stood up on his hind legs," my grandmother told us, bending her hands at the wrist to illustrate a dinosaur standing up on its hind legs. "He looked over his shoulder at us and made this strange sound, like a roaring sound but small, then took off for the burnie-can." The burnie-can, I should explain, was a rusted oil drum that my grandfather used to burn things in, back in a time when burning things was an acceptable way of getting rid of them. There were holes and tears in the side of this can and toward the bottom, from repeated exposure to fire and the elements, and apparently the dinosaur ran in through one of those openings. "We didn't know what to do," my mother cut in. "The dinosaur was in the burnie-can!"

Little by little we got the story of how, with great caution, my mother and grandmother decided to overturn the burnie-can, clothes basket once more at the ready. But when they followed through with their plan, the dinosaur was gone.

No one that evening quite knew what to make of my mother and grandmother's story, and even my father, who had a mean streak and loved any opportunity to ridicule, was unusually reserved. Nobody, it was clear by the time the blueberry cobbler was on the table, knew what to say. As kids we were used to telling stories that had a heightened sense of what was possible. (One time, sitting alone in the basement, my sister Ailie swore she'd seen a small parade of ghosts, and ghosts of rabbits at that, spirits of dead animals that my grandfather had hunted and then skinned at a long low porcelain sink.) That the grownups were telling a story this strange and improbable was exhilarating and frightening at the same time.

Several times more the ladies alternated with their descriptions of the prehistoric creature. It stood on two feet, but it had another set of little feet that it kept tucked close to its puffed-up chest. It was as green, my grandmother added, as the ginger ale bottle that was sitting on the table in front of us. It had a long toothy snout and a tiny red tongue that lashed out in quick, furtive movements, and a long slender tail that it seemed to use not only for balance but for propulsion.

Finally my sister went into the living room and returned with the volume of an encyclopedia that identified the dinosaur. It was a miniature *Tyrannosaurus rex*. The illustration in the reference book seemed to be all the proof the ladies needed that what they had seen was real. Everybody got up from the table except for my grandfather, who sat there for a long time by himself, pipe in one hand, the silver-plated lighter my grandmother had given him that past Christmas in the other.

My mother put the dishes into the sink. My grandmother went into the living room to lie down. My sister and I wandered around the house and then out into the yard. My father took the shotgun from the basement and went out back. What he did, on balmy summer evenings such as this one, was to sit out in a lawn chair and shoot rats as they emerged at dusk from the woodpile on the far side of the property. He got a kick out of it, and nobody in the family seemed very eager to speak up for the rats, and in those days neighbors didn't seem to object very much to a man shooting off a sixteen-gauge shotgun in his own backyard. He'd take a can of beer out with him, a pack of Lucky Strikes rolled up in the sleeve of his T-shirt, and the blasting would be done in an hour. He killed them with my grandfather's shotgun, a pump-action Browning that is no longer in the family. The rats exploded off the top of the pile, and each time my father hit one he laughed and cried out in the manner of Edward G. Robinson in *Little Caesar*: "Mother of mercy! Is this the end of Rico?"

Sometimes my sister and I would sit on the back porch and watch him, sheets of Kleenex wadded in our ears and drooping down on our shoulders so that we looked, as my mother liked to observe, like a pair of precious bunnyrabbits. Other times, if we had a little money, we'd walk the two blocks to the Dairy Queen. In either case the shooting was over by nine o'clock, at which time we had to get ready for bed, school night or not. The procedure was that we'd get in our pajamas, each one of us in our own bed, and then my father would come in and spank us. The spankings varied with my father's mood, but we had one every night, as he liked to say, whether we needed it or not. He used his right hand, and sometimes his calfskin belt, doubled up to create a lot of noise and a little sharp sting through the thin summer bedclothes. When it was over Ailie and I would both be bawling our heads off and laughing simultaneously, a sort of emotional confusion that was a cross between the shame that accompanies senseless violence and the exhilarating silliness stirred up by a pillow fight.

My father would wish us good night and my mother would come and tuck us in, following which we might coax a story out of our grandfather. On this night my grandfather told us that there was no story that could top the one we'd heard at dinner, so the lights were turned out and we drifted off to sleep, as I'd like to remember, dreaming of bottle-green, fiery-tongued dinosaurs.

This day that I've described would be unimportant, of course, if not for the dinosaur story, which stayed in the family the way a good service of dishes does, or a first class recipe, and was trotted out on special occasions. When enough time had elapsed that people would not be quite so prone to point fingers or talk behind their hands, first my father and then various family members told the story in front of friends and neighbors, and in time the story got around and acquired something of a reputation. People seemed to like the idea that such a thing was possible; my mother and grandmother were known to be simple, truthful women, and there really was the possibility that they'd seen a dinosaur, or at least a creature that exactly resembled one. People also had the added enjoyment of thinking up various explanations. It was a lizard or something that had escaped from a pet shop. Then too, maybe it really was a dinosaur.

Invariably there also followed the story of my father's scheme of capturing the dinosaur and getting rich in some way by his ownership of it. He had, later that evening when we were fast asleep, read the description in the encyclopedia, which said that Mr. *Tyrannosaurus rex* was a carnivore, a meat eater. My father reasoned that the dead rats by the woodpile would be too much for the little fellow to resist, and that if he just kept his eyes open he could capture an early retirement with the possibility of an appearance on Johnny Carson or Merv Griffin. He even devised a snare, using an old crab trap, but it never came to anything.

The mysterious sighting, though, worked no end of change on our little family. For one thing, my father didn't come in to spank us any longer. Neither my sister nor I ever had the urge to ask him why. And my mother seemed to get off the diet pills, too, though she got fat as a result—for a time she was plump as Santa, and just as jolly—and spent a lot of time baking. Pop, always nice, was still nice. He still shot rabbits now and then, but only he and my father would eat them. My grandmother, who'd passed a good part of the last twenty years in a prone position, rising only for the few household chores she liked to do, started to get up and around more. Her only son had died in the Second World War, I should mention, and it had ruined her outlook. The sighting of the dinosaur was somehow restorative, though nobody ever figured out how.

This is a story of my childhood and how I remember my childhood. Happy times went on in this way for quite some time; in my heart I chalked it up to the good luck brought to our house by the dinosaur. The other shoe did drop, though, and that also had to do with the dinosaur. It started to get around that my father was having an affair with the girl who worked the register at the auto parts store where he spent a fair amount of his leisure time. My mother confided this to me, suddenly, in the middle of a silent August afternoon; the only thing you could hear was the sound of the cicadas, buzzing like an electrical current in the overgrown buttonwood trees. She wanted to know if I thought she should leave my father because of it, and even though it came as a small surprise that an adult should be asking a child for advice on a subject like this, it wasn't so difficult for me to answer that she should. I think I shocked her, as if she suddenly saw a whole new part of me she'd never dreamed existed. "You can do better," I told her in a world-weary voice. "You can do a whole lot better."

She never did, though, and my father's affairs and my mother's forbearance in the face of them became sort of legendary around town. Women who would not have normally had anything to do with him lined up, one after the other; it was as if he'd suddenly discovered a magical power and become someone else, someone he had been all the while trying to become and then had, at the very last, become. Most people, I've found, do not become what they have all the while secretly planned on becoming, and it tickled my father that he'd been able to get it right. This too gave my mother a more interesting role, which she cherished; she found herself all the more valuable because she was the one who could lay legitimate claim to a man who'd ended up, by the mid-seventies, wearing Italian sports jackets and driving a two-tone aqua and pearl '63 Thunderbird convertible.

If all this seems a bit unsavory, I should add that he also became a kind and loving man, and never hit us again, and never shot another rat again, as far as I know. Another person had emerged, though he came into the world with a fairly high price tag dangling from his sleeve.

The next incident that makes up this rather loosely constructed narrative has to do with a man who used to come to the house once each year, either on his way to or returning from a lake in Canada where he said the most beautiful and delicious trout in the world existed. This man, whose name was Robert Welsh, had been my Uncle Buddy's bunkmate in the Marines, in 1943, in the Second World War. They had been eighteen-year-old kids together, and had gone through boot camp together, and had been shipped to the Pacific Theater together. At some juncture in their brief friendship they had also struck the promise that if one of them died the other would look in on the dead soldier's parents. My Uncle Buddy, as it turns out, was the one who'd perished, in a matter of a few months, in some skirmish in the South Pacific on a spit of sand that didn't even have a name.

The day the government man came to the house is also an important story. It took place on another one of those silent sweltering August afternoons. The man in his dark suit came into the driveway in his polished dark car, its bulbous chrome fenders gleaming. Pop was sitting out on the front porch counting the minutes until it would be dinnertime while Nan was out in the kitchen, placing a blueberry cobbler into the pie safe. My mother was upstairs, writing a letter to her brother on stationery she'd bought that very afternoon. The writing paper was powder blue and featured a little reproduction of the ceiling of the Sistine Chapel at the very top of the page, the part where God and man touch the ends of their fingers together.

In the mythology of our family the government man comes into the house and Nan drops the pie before he can even say what he came to our house to say. Pop shows him out. There is a heavy crashing, and mom in her room knows what has happened without having to go downstairs to ask any questions. Meanwhile, there has been a fly buzzing furiously at the top corner of her open window. She takes her shoes off and stands up on the chair. She traps the fly by rolling the writing paper into a cone pressed against the glass, climbs down from the chair, and sits once more at her writing desk; then, the fly in her fingers, she pulls its wings off one at a time. In this way, my mother told me one day when we were having one of our secret conversations, she sat by herself in her little upstairs room, watching the wingless fly wander the ceiling of the Sistine Chapel for a few minutes before balling up the sheet of stationery and wadding it into the back of her desk drawer.

No one said anything, about my Uncle Buddy or anything else. My grandmother took to her bed for many years. My grandfather doted on his wife, and on his little girl. A few years later my mother brought home a taxi driver she'd met on her way home from school. Not even a year later they were married, and at approximately the same time I was born.

But I see I've wandered away from the subject of my Uncle Buddy's bunkmate Robert Welsh. He came by our house each year, on his way either to or from Quebec Province, and I watched him come and go, and enjoyed it, from an early age. It was something to look forward to, like a national holiday, for Robert Welsh always carried in the backseat of his car extravagant gifts of whiskey and cigarettes, chocolate bars and frivolous toys and novelties presented in fancy packages at a time of year when Christmas seemed as if it would never come again—the seasons of childhood are so long and slow. I remember him in automobiles of different makes and models, always new, always well cared for, coming to our house always with different women, I don't think ever the same one twice, some of them girlfriends and some wives, albeit extremely short-term wives, in about equal proportion. He had fast cars and convertible cars and long cars and expensive serious cars. He was at first handsome and glib and then filled out and a bit preposterous and then finally alcoholic and flush-faced and tired-seeming, suffering from angina. It was always a point of interest to see what he would be like on his next visit, what the woman would be like, what the car would be like.

The only thing that never varied was that he would always have to tell the story of the day my Uncle Buddy was blown up. There was the usual bourbon-induced rollercoaster of emotions that led up to this point, and this point in the visit to him possibly was the point. Everybody saw that he had to tell this story, that he'd come to our house in order to tell it, and continued to come in order to tell it, again and again. There was a beach on some tiny nameless Pacific island and a chaotic landing on that beach and then a lot of smoke and men screaming and shouting and then a heavy deep blast like someone had punched him in the stomach and then he was up and running with my uncle, only he'd gotten it backwards, or not quite right: it was just Uncle Buddy's leg he was carrying under his arm. That was the last Robert saw of my Uncle Buddy, his right leg, his green pant-leg, his high black boot with its metal-tipped lace.

We knew when Robert told the story of the leg that he would be gone the next morning, and he always was, until the next year when he would come to our house without warning and then leave once more without warning. It was the dinosaur, once again, that seemed to change things, because Nan after all that time had finally begun to get up and around, and many years later, on her deathbed, she still wondered if she had done the right thing by telling Robert Welsh never to come to her house again, he was no longer welcome, she was tired of seeing ghosts.

All this has an end, the story has an end, if not exactly a plot. Our lives went on the way lives go on. My father became more profligate, though everyone always forgave him because he had found this nice way to be. It's what everybody said about my father, that he had a nice way about him. My mother meanwhile went back to the prescription drugs and the soap operas, cigarettes and speed all the livelong afternoon. She was a very speedy ma, right up until the day when she discovered Valium, that is, at which time she became a very languorous ma. My sister and I grew up all the same. Pop was good to us, and took us out in the pine forest for long walks with his beagles, and he even stopped shooting rabbits when my sister Ailie finally asked him to. My grandmother continued to spoil my mother and treat her like a child; in this the story of Uncle Buddy also figures. When Nan disappeared my mother disappeared as well, at least for a time.

That was on the day of my grandmother's funeral. She'd had a long and bitter fight with emphysema, sneaking cigarettes to the very end. She was the only woman my grandfather had ever developed an interest in, as he occasionally enjoyed pointing out to us, ever since the day he'd spotted her out in a field, all by herself, picking dahlias. She was not doing this for beauty or for idleness; she was getting paid one cent per dahlia. I like to think of two people who met and fell in love in summertime, not too long after the First World War, in a dahlia field. I like to think of a time when there was such a thing as a dahlia field. Maybe there still is, but I've never seen one.

So this story starts someplace in the early twenties, with two people standing talking in a dahlia field, and this story ends on the day of my grandmother's funeral in the late autumn or early winter of 1985. There are some stops along the way, like the incident that happened perhaps ten years after the courtship in the dahlia field. Pop owned land, with his two brothers, and they split it up and the three of them went to work, building three houses from one set of plans. My grandfather, in this way, came to own his house free and clear, and settled there, and fathered first a son and then a daughter. When the Great Depression arrived there was a man in the town named Ward Lyons who was going around trying to buy up everything cheap. This kind of character is a cliché in the movies, but in the real life of my grandfather and our little town he made a very good and original villain. When he came to our house Pop greeted him with a loaded shotgun—the same one that has been featured elsewhere in this story—a gallon of gasoline, and these words: "Ward, I will burn this house to the ground before you ever get your hands on it." This was a story told often in the family because my grandfather had never acted that way before, and he had never acted that way again. An important moment in his life had come and he'd responded to it honorably. He wouldn't tell the story himself but my grandmother told it for him, many times, complete with dialogue and stage directions. It was repeated much more than the dinosaur story, but it was similar, in a way. It was a story about something that mattered.

There are other stories that could be included, stories about things that mattered, that matter still; the last one, as I've already said, takes place on the day of my grandmother's funeral. My mother during this time was admitted into the hospital for certain tendencies she'd been exhibiting, tendencies that featured sleeping pills and razor blades, for the reason that after all those years my father had finally left her. So it was only the three of us who went in the rented black limousine to the cemetery, my grandfather in the front seat, my sister and me in the back. We watched the coffin as it was lowered, and we tossed red roses after it as it went deeper into the ground. It was a misty, colorless afternoon, the first day of December. On the other side of the graveyard, perched rather dramatically on a wheel-rutted hill, my father sat by himself in his '63 Thunderbird, smoking a cigarette and wearing a trench coat and a pair of wraparound sunglasses. He was not mocking us, I don't think; my grandmother had been good to him and he was, after his own fashion, paying his last respects. At least that is what I told myself and that is what I tried to tell my sister Ailie. We did our best to keep my grandfather from noticing him, but of course he did.

"Wait on that," Pop said, pulling ferociously at his necktie and generally losing patience with the stiffness of his black polyester suit. "Just wait on that."

Nothing more was said. After the funeral we went back to the house and had a country-style buffet supper. Women from our town brought delicious things to eat in covered dishes and gigantic Tupperware bowls, deviled eggs and cold fried chicken and baked bean casseroles topped with slabs of crispy bacon. The house was as full of life and companionship as I have ever seen it, friends and neighbors and family members with connections going back generations, in many of those people the characteristic chin of my grandmother's side, the small frame and thinning hair of my grandfather's. Pop passed the afternoon in his sitting room, framed by his collection of pipes arranged in built-in shelves on the wall behind his La-Z-Boy, simultaneously telling stories of rabbit hunts and chicken fights and his two dead brothers who'd distilled moonshine and watching his favorite show, *The Wheel of Fortune*. People do not think of these activities as associated with New Jersey (hunting rabbits and fighting roosters and mixing up moonshine, I mean—not watching *The Wheel of Fortune*) but there are many things about southern New Jersey that are on the verge of being forgotten. A lot of us are country people and we were raised country; now all the farmland is gone, or most of it, and an awful lot of the pine forest too, and the state of New Jersey seems to be not much more than a gigantic strip mall. But on that day my grandfather advanced the opinion that life is not just what you see in front of you but everything that has happened. History, in his view, was taking place all at once. It's probably because of this that the dinosaur came up, and even though everybody present had heard the account in all its variations, no one objected to hearing it again. It was like those stories of the Jersey Devil, only better because of the unimpeachable character of the witnesses, and even after all that time people talked and argued about the dinosaur as if the sighting had taken place that very afternoon, and there were even a few other people, as it turned out, who claimed to have gotten a glimpse of it.

That story, plus a few too many highballs, conspired to put my grandfather in a certain mood. When all the friends and relatives finally left, including my sister Ailie, who was then just out of high school and living crosstown with her boyfriend Artie—a twisty young dice dealer from Atlantic City who had convinced Ailie to give up her scholarship to NYU for a life of PASSION—Pop took me down into the basement where we stood for a moment at the long low sink at which he'd skinned and gutted the rabbits. He told me that he'd salvaged that sink when the asbestos company he'd worked for was getting ready to remodel their lavatory: the rabbit sink, it turned out, had been a men's urinal. He showed me also that he'd saved the collars of all his beagles and had them in a velvet-lined Christmas box. Next to that, tangled together inside a Folger's can, were the metal spurs that the high-spirited young men had attached to the feet of the fighting roosters. From there we went to the brass-trimmed footlocker that contained the flag taken from Uncle Buddy's coffin, and also his dress blues, and his letters from home, and the journal he'd kept in the short space between boot camp and the end of his life.

Also in the basement, suspended on two mismatched coat hooks above the sink, was Pop's sixteen gauge shotgun, the one he'd used to hunt rabbits and game birds, the one my father had used to exterminate rats. This gun my grandfather loaded, his fingers feeding the red shells one at a time into the underside of the rifle, for he wanted to go out back and have a little fun of an autumn evening. He wanted to blow off a little steam, he explained, and talk some more about the olden days.

It's a strange accident that, as we went up the steps and then out onto the back porch, my father was just stepping out of his car and then for a moment as if to regain his balance standing by the burnie-can with a long-handled white wicker basketful of dahlias, and just as strange that even as he opened his mouth as if to greet us my grandfather pulled the trigger of the shotgun. No words were exchanged. Earlier that day, as I'd helped him on with his suit coat, Pop told me that his only regret was letting my father into his house. "I knowed what he was," Pop kept insisting to me. "I knowed what he was." What my father was back then, we all knew, was a taxi driver who liked to troll the side streets for high school girls. He'd finally gotten one and, typical of his lot, had cast her aside, even though it had taken him more than twenty years to do it. Pop was defending his daughter's lost honor, you might say, regardless of how long it had taken for her to lose it or for him to get around to defending it.

My grandfather's eyesight was poor, but he did manage to clip my father in the arm that held the basket of flowers. You can imagine the terrible ordeal that followed, legal and otherwise, so I won't bother to go into all that here. It's a mess at the end, a king-sized mess, as the story of any family would be, I suppose, if you only had enough information, and if the story only went on long enough. The only thing that might somehow square everything up, of course, would be the return of the dinosaur. Perhaps that's what you've been waiting for, and I'm happy not to disappoint you because within the collection of stories that makes up the history of my family the dinosaur does make a final, unforgettable appearance. My father and grandfather saw it, I saw it, we all saw it. And to this very day we tell people about the spilled basket of parti-colored flowers, the paint-peeled house, the front yard with its rusted, dented can—my grandfather with the shotgun in his hand and my poor father rolling and thrashing on the ground, his spiffy new car still idling—a million-year-old creature emerging from a jagged tear at the bottom of the burnie-can, stopping just long enough for us to see that he is, in fact, a dinosaur, then moving off with great dignity across the open field.

Acknowledgments

For all their encouragement and support, many thanks to my mother and brother, Collene and Jim Moxford, Brian and Linda Cruse, Chris Walsh, Bill Marx, Sharon Portnoff, Michael Degener, Michael Prince, Maria Zlateva, Kim Shuckra-Gomez, James Pasto, Mary McGowan, Salvatore Sciabona, Keith Botsford, Janet Tracy Landman, Mike Remshard, and especially to my teachers, Leslie Epstein and Fr. Anthony I. McHale, S. J.

The following stories have been previously published, and changes have been made to them since their initial publication: "The Old Priest," *2013 Pushcart Prize XXXVII: Best of the Small Presses*, edited by Bill Henderson (Wainscott: Pushcart, 2013); "The Old Priest," *Republic of Letters* 22 (Spring 2011), http://mag.trolbooks.com/2011/04/the-old-priest/; "The City of Gold" as "Pueblo," *236* (Fall 2005), http://wwwbu.edu/writing/236 (*236* is the e-magazine of Boston University's Graduate Creative Writing Program); "Snow behind the Door," *Another Chicago Magazine*, Spring 2003; "The Unexamined Life," *CutBank*, Fall 2001; "Jack Frost," *Sou'wester* (Summer 1998); and "Upstairs Room," *New Millennium Writings* (Summer 1998).